walking backward

CATHERINE AUSTEN

ORCA BOOK PUBLISHERS

Library and Archives Canada Cataloguing in Publication

Austen, Catherine, 1965-
Walking backward / written by Catherine Austen.

ISBN 978-1-55469-147-0

I. Title.

PS8601.U785W34 2009   jC813'.6   C2009-902804-2

First published in the United States, 2009
Library of Congress Control Number: 2009928210

Summary: After his mother dies in a phobia-related car crash,
twelve-year-old Josh tries to make sense of his grief while he looks after
his little brother and watches his father retreat into a fantasy world.

Orca Book Publishers gratefully acknowledges the support for its publishing
programs provided by the following agencies: the Government of Canada through
the Book Publishing Industry Development Program and the Canada Council for the
Arts, and the Province of British Columbia through the BC Arts Council
and the Book Publishing Tax Credit.

Design by Teresa Bubela
Cover artwork by Dreamstime
Author photo by Melinda Vallillee

ORCA BOOK PUBLISHERS
PO Box 5626, STN. B
VICTORIA, BC CANADA
V8R 6S4

ORCA BOOK PUBLISHERS
PO Box 468
CUSTER, WA USA
98240-0468

www.orcabook.com
Printed and bound in Canada.
Printed on 100% PCW recycled paper.
12 11 10 09 • 4 3 2 1

For my children, Sawyer and Daimon,
and my mother, Mary.

Monday, July 30th

My father is insane. He just came home from his appointment with the psychiatrist and handed me this journal. "You have to keep track of your feelings in this, Josh!" he shouted. Then he went into the basement to work on his time machine.

Dad only shouted so I could hear him over my music. He never shouts because he's angry. He doesn't get angry. I'm pretty sure he's a cyborg. If Mom had walked into my room, she'd have shouted in anger. Not that she shouted often, but at that moment my friend Simpson was shoving a safety pin through my eyebrow, and I was bleeding down my face and neck. Mom would have had a fit. Dad could walk in and see body parts hanging from the ceiling and not raise an eyebrow.

I opened the journal to see if Dad had written any words of wisdom to get me started. Just as I turned the cover, two drops of blood dripped from my face onto the first page. They were perfect, sort of splattery and dark red, so I left the page blank. I think Dr. Tierney will appreciate the symbolism. He'll probably schedule an extra session to talk about it.

I finally got my face to stop bleeding, but now I can't get the ring in my eyebrow. I don't think the hole goes all the way through. That's just as well, because I don't actually like pierced brows. If your hair is too long, the ring gets snagged on your comb. If your hair is too short, you can't hide the hole when it gets infected. My hair is medium length—long enough for snagging but too short for hiding. It's guaranteed I'll develop a gross festering sore where my eyebrow used to be unless I let the hole close over right now. I only let Simpson do it because he said he was good at piercing, and I lost at Rock Paper Scissors, which is very out of character for me because I almost always win.

Simpson went home after he stabbed the safety pin halfway into his own thumb. I guess he lied about his piercing skills.

I like the way this journal feels. Mom used to give me notebooks for my story ideas and drawings, but they were always cheap dollar-store books like the kind she kept her own notes in. This one is fancier.

Dr. Tierney tucked in a photocopied article about using a journal to track your feelings. I'm supposed to treat it like an emotional database. After I've used it for a while, I can check what I was feeling on any given day and calculate how many times a week I get angry.

I don't think it'll track my feelings properly, because if I'm happy I'm not going to run to my journal. You only write in a journal when you're too miscrable to do anything else. So this will probably be full of sad thoughts. Then when I check back on my emotional database, I'll think I was sad all the time, when actually I'm not. But maybe I'll become sad all the time because my journal says everything sucks, when actually it doesn't. This journal could ruin my life. But the article doesn't say that. It says I should write every day to work through my grief.

Dr. Tierney scribbled a note on the article: *It's very important to write every time you have a strong feeling, Josh, and review the journal each week.* So when someone makes me laugh or cry, I'm supposed to say, "Hey, man, I've got a strong feeling coming on," and rush off to write it down. It's supposed to be private, but Dad will probably sneak into my room to read it. Then he'll think I'm sad all the time, and that will turn him into a sad person too. Seriously, this thing is dangerous.

Dad got his own journal from Dr. Tierney but, since Dad doesn't have emotions, I can't see what he'll use it for except time-travel theories. Ever since Mom died, he's been obsessed with building a time machine. I asked him, "Why? So you can go back to when she was alive and ignore her some more?" He didn't find that funny. But it didn't make him angry either. He just looked confused, same as always.

Dad's the sort of nerd who might actually succeed in building a time machine. One day I'll walk down to the basement, and Dad will be gone. Sammy and I will be orphans. We'll be split up and sent to abusive homes. I'll be shipped to farm country, where some creepy foster father will use me for slave labor. Sammy will be herded into an orphanage, where they'll tease him about his stutter and turn him into an avenging psychopath.

As far as I know, Dad's time-travel obsession came totally out of the blue. I've never seen him pick up a science book in my life. He works in a government office where they make maps. It would be exciting to explore the world and draw maps of what you found. But that's not what Dad does. He sits at a computer and types in information he gets from satellite pictures and other people. That sounds boring. But who knows? Maybe he met an explorer from the future, or maybe he saw a hole in the fabric of the universe, because for some reason he honestly thinks he has a shot at building a time machine. Which I'm guessing he'll use to go back to the day Mom died and stop her from taking the car.

I asked him yesterday how his time-travel plans were going. He flashed a smile and said, "Couldn't be better, Josh." His eyes sparkled like he was an inch away from a wormhole. When he's at work tomorrow, I might sneak a peek at his journal to see what's going on in his head. They still let him go to work despite his obvious insanity.

Dr. Tierney gave Dad a notebook for Sammy too. Since Sam's four and a half and the only letter he can write is *S*, I don't think it's going to be an effective therapy for him. Mom taught me to read and write before I started kindergarten, but she said that left me nothing to learn in school, so I turned naughty out of boredom. She made a special effort to keep Sammy as uneducated as possible.

I'm part boy, part experiment. Mom was a professor of epic literature in the medieval studies department of the university, and she turned me into a freak by reading me *Beowulf* and *The Song of Roland* instead of letting me vegetate in front of *Caillou* and *Ninja Turtles*. Some of what she taught me required me to learn French and German. For other stuff I had to read the Bible, the Greek myths and ancient history. I'm a bit advanced for my age, which is twelve. Fortunately, I'm an excellent soccer player so I'm not a total geek.

My friends like it that I know about history and mythology, but with adults I pretend I don't know so much. Grown-ups don't like kids with classical educations. "No one likes a know-it-all," my mom used to say. I tell my teachers I learned everything from computer games.

On the upside, I am the player to fear in *Civilization*, *Age of Empires*, *Age of Mythology* and even *Call of Duty*, which I can play now that Mom's not here to monitor game ratings, and Dad's too busy on his time machine to notice if I'm even home. On the downside, I actually like history, but there's no one to talk to about it other than creepy chat-room people lurking in wait for underage overachievers.

Sammy will never have to face this dilemma. Instead of *Sir Gawain and the Green Knight*, he got Mother Goose and Teletoon. And every spare minute of Mom's time.

Sammy just walked into my room a second ago. He's jumping on my bed. I have the best bed for jumping in our house. Sam's ceiling is sloped, so he smashes his head if he jumps on his own bed. That doesn't stop him from jumping on it every afternoon before smashing his head and then coming into my room to jump on my bed. Mom and Dad have a futon, so it's not very bouncy. Plus the cats are usually asleep on it. I have a double mattress and a nine-foot ceiling, so a kid Sam's size can catch some truly awesome air.

I can't bounce so high because I'm five feet tall. Which is not tall for my age, but I'm good at basketball anyway. I'll be thirteen on February 10. I'm in grade seven. Or I will be when school starts in September.

Before Mom died, I was excited about going into grade seven. The junior high school is huge, with a swimming pool and two soccer fields and an auditorium separate from the gym. Now I'm not looking forward to school so much. Once your mother dies, you're either unhappy because your mother died, or you're happy but you think you shouldn't be because your mother just died, or you're happy and not thinking about it until other people look at you like you're a freak for being happy when your mother just died. Any way you look at it, it's not happy.

On the upside, you can do things you ordinarily wouldn't be allowed to do—like pierce your eyebrow—because everyone thinks it's a reaction to your mother's death. Sammy and I have been staying up till eleven every night, wearing our pajamas all day long and spending our outdoor time destroying the walnut tree in the backyard by whacking it with plastic swords. We've broken almost all our swords over the past month, and we had quite a collection. The neighbors walk by and see us attacking the tree in our jammies, and they just wave. So that's the upside.

The downside is that everyone thinks they know what you're feeling, but they're usually wrong. If somebody ticks you off, they'll say, "I know you're angry because your mother died," when really it's like, "No, I'm angry because you ticked me off."

The worst downside is that your mom's dead.

Right now Sammy is bugging me, asking, "Can I play *Scooby-Doo*?" That means he wants to sit beside me while I play his video game. He's addicted to Scooby-Doo—the show, the movies, the board game, the books. He has Scooby-Doo jigsaw puzzles and doodle bags and coloring books. Half the things he says are quotations from Fred and Velma. When I look at Sammy, I understand how I learned so much when I was young. When *Scooby-Doo* comes on TV, he can tell right away which episode it is. From one camera shot, he knows. He has all the mysteries and monsters catalogued in his mind. It's like this amazing mental potential gone wrong.

Mom got him the PlayStation game *Scooby-Doo! Mystery Mayhem*, but Sam can't play it. He can't press the controls quickly enough. He's too scared. He can't handle the ghosts and zombies, even when I'm playing it. He screams and patters his feet on the ground as if he's running away, when really he's sitting on his butt. And it's not like it's ever game over for Scooby and Shaggy. I don't know why he's so scared. But he's less afraid of Scooby-Doo than just about anything else in the world.

Dr. Tierney says that being afraid of everything is a normal reaction to Mom dying. But Sammy has *always* been afraid of everything. Except snakes and spiders and mice, which normal people are afraid of. Sam loves them. He's afraid of everything else: darkness, dogs, crowds, elevators, escalators, steak knives, swimming pools, old people, little girls. You name it, he's afraid of it. Mom used to lie down with him after story time because he was too scared to be in his bed alone. I gave her a hard time about that, but she said she was the same when she was little and had to go to bed before her sister. So she lay with Sammy until he fell asleep. I told her she was spoiling him, because he had to learn to do it on his own, but she said no. She said, "He needs to know I'll always be there to protect him."

So much for that theory.

Since Mom died, exactly one month ago, Sam has been staying up with me at night. If I'm doing something scary, like watching anything other than *Scooby-Doo*, he'll sit in the basement with Dad. I don't think it's right for a four-year-old to hang out with a grown-up who thinks he's building a time machine. But what do I know about kids just because I am one?

Sammy is screaming in terror right now. Cleo, our cat, was sleeping under the covers, and Sam just bounced on her. She's fine, but he's scared half to death.

Thursday, August 2nd

I missed a couple of journal days already, so Dr. Tierney will be disappointed. I don't remember if I had any strong emotions. I know Sammy did—he had a fit in the bath last night.

I got his tub ready like Mom used to, with the bathmat and bubbles and toys. He sat down and started playing, but when he found a toy car under the suds, he went crazy—screaming and splashing and nearly drowning himself. He threw the car so hard he knocked over the toothbrush cup, and all our toothbrushes fell in the toilet. I got mad and started yelling, and I made him cry.

It's the most awful feeling in the world, when you lose your temper and swear and make a four-year-old cry. What kind of person yells at a four-year-old kid?

Mom only yelled at Sammy if he picked up one of the cats by the back leg. Dad saves his screams for life-and-death situations like playing on the road. What else could you possibly do when you're only four that would be so bad you should be yelled at?

Actually, there are some rotten four-year-olds out there. There's a kid at the park who hits other kids and throws sand in their faces and steals their toys. His name is Darren. At first I thought he was retarded, but then I realized that he likes to hurt people. Animals too. Once he ran after a squirrel with his plastic shovel, chasing it across the grass until it ran up a tree. He stared up after it and whacked the tree about a hundred times, shouting, "This is what I'll do to you!" As if the squirrel might have been unclear about his intentions.

I can see how some four-year-olds might deserve to be yelled at. Or in Darren's case, locked up. Darren's mom just sits there, smoking and talking on her phone like she doesn't care at all that her kid hits other kids and tries to kill helpless animals. Darren would have to chop off someone's head to get her attention. Somebody should yell at him before he does that.

But I shouldn't have yelled at Sammy last night. He's a good boy. The only reason he freaked out was because I accidentally put a car in his bath.

Sammy has freaked out over cars ever since he learned how Mom died. He thinks the car killed her. We've explained a million times, but he doesn't get it. He's so afraid of cars he won't even sit in one anymore. We should have lied and said Mom died bungee jumping or mountain climbing. Then he'd be afraid of extreme sports and he could still lead a normal life.

Being afraid of cars is very limiting in the modern world. We live in the suburbs, and everything is too far to walk to. I'm okay with my bike, but Sam with his training wheels goes about half a kilometer an hour. There's a bus—which in Sam's head doesn't count as an evil car—but it only comes by our house once an hour. It comes more often during rush hour, but then it's crowded with grown-ups who try to squeeze into a seat with us. As if kids don't qualify for the one-person-per-seat rule. Somebody always looks at Sammy and asks, "Can't he shove over a little?"

I've started wearing Mom's old watch so we can catch the hourly bus if we need to. It's not a girly watch. It's the one she wore swimming. It's black, with a timer I don't know how to work. It looks good on me, and it'll help us make the bus if we ever go anywhere.

Dad doesn't take us anywhere because he's emotionally absent, which is Dr. Tierney's term for living in a daze. Dad is stuck in the first stage of grief, called denial and isolation. The next stages are anger, bargaining, and depression—I don't want to see Dad go through those. Sammy combines all the stages into one emotional tornado. He zones out, he yells, he cries, he comes up with ideas to get Mom back, he yells some more, he cries some more, he zones out. It's exhausting just watching him.

The last stage of grief is called acceptance. I can't see any of us ever getting that far. But it would be nice if Dad came out of the basement once in a while and took us out to eat. We may be grieving, but we still have basic needs. Dr. Tierney says Dad will snap out of his daze eventually. I don't think it helps to let him hide in the basement with delusions of time travel. But I haven't gone to medical school to learn how to tell people it's okay to neglect their children, so what do I know?

I can't wait until I'm old enough to drive myself around. I love cars as much as Sammy hates them. I try not to think of the accident, of course. When I see a car like Mom's—one of those Subaru Outbacks that old people drive—I get a chill like it might be her, only shorter with white hair and glasses. But I understand that it wasn't the car that killed her. It was her crazy fear of snakes.

That sounds strange. How could a snake cause a car accident? You'd think maybe she swerved into a tree trying to avoid a snake or something. But no. The snake was actually inside the car, and she freaked out when she saw it. Mom had a snake phobia.

A couple of years ago, when we visited Toronto, there was a picture of a snake on the subway. Mom saw it and ran to another car. She opened the doors while the train was moving and took off, screaming, while Dad sat there, embarrassed, trying to keep me and Sammy in our seats. Mom waved at us from the next car. She calmed down once she got away from the picture.

Phobias are serious things. I'm glad I don't have any. Snakes creep me out, but I wouldn't run off a moving subway train to get away from one. And I wouldn't drive off a highway into a tree if there was one in my car. I'd just pull over and get out.

We don't know how the snake got inside Mom's car. The trunk was open for a while, but we live in the suburbs, not the jungle, and garter snakes don't climb trees and dangle down through sunroofs. So it's a mystery where it came from.

A garden spider once came in through the sunroof. It was the size of my fist, with thick legs and a big abdomen marked like a face. I didn't notice it at first because it blended so well into the upholstery. Mom was buckling Sammy into his booster chair beside me when Sam said, "Hey look! It's a spider."

I thought he might have seen a daddy longlegs or something normal-sized. But no. There was a spider on steroids stretched on the back of the driver's seat, dead center, six inches from Sammy's knee.

Mom nearly had a heart attack. At first she was like, "Oh yeah? Where's the spider, honey?" I could tell she was expecting the kind of little spider you see every day. She looked where Sam pointed, and she nearly jumped a foot. She was all, "Okay. Oh my god. Look at the size of it. Okay." She went to get something to catch it in, because she never killed spiders or any kind of bug. She asked if Sammy wanted to stay in his seat—because he was already buckled in and everything—and he said, "Sure!" like it was the greatest thing to be strapped down next to a giant spider. This is the kid terrified of Chihuahuas and Batman. I was out of the car by then. There's no way I would stay in a car with a spider that size.

Mom came back with a jar. As soon as she held it up, the spider jumped to the bottom of the glass. It must have been a very cool and frightening sight from Sammy's point of view. He would have seen the spider make a leap straight for him, then stop in midair when it hit the glass. Mom slid a piece of cardboard over the jar, and the spider started scrambling around looking for a way out. She called me over and said, "Listen." I could hear the spider's legs on the glass as it moved. Really fast clicks, *tchicka-tchicka-tchick*, like a horror movie.

Mom kept the sunroof closed after that, so that's not how the snake got in the car. The day she died, she had just driven home with groceries before she went out again, so she might have left the trunk open while she carried in the bags. But I don't think a snake climbed inside. Snakes are afraid of cars. I figure someone put the snake there on purpose. Maybe they knew Mom had a phobia and they wanted her to crash the car, and it wasn't an accident at all. That's what the police thought at first. But they gave up trying to figure out who did it. They ruled it an accident. I'm still looking for a better answer.

It's hard to explain to people about Mom's phobia. Everyone thinks, "Why did she ram her car into a tree?" And the answer, "Because there was a snake in the car and she spazzed out," isn't a good answer. Sometimes I tell people the car went out of control because of mechanical difficulties. But it didn't. She just drove into a tree.

I'm afraid she'll get a Darwin Award for this. There's a group called the Darwin Society that gives awards to people who die doing stupid things. Their stupidity caused their death, so it's like natural selection.

Of course, the dead person isn't around to accept the award—but who would want an award for being incredibly stupid?

For example, a school bus broke down during an animal-safari field trip. The bus was like a cage that kept the visitors safe while tigers and baboons roamed free outside it. The class had been warned to stay in their seats and not to leave the vehicle for any reason. But the driver went out to fix the bus anyway. The tigers killed him. They went straight for his throat. He won a Darwin Award because that's a stupid way to die.

But I don't think it's all that stupid. Imagine being stuck in a bus full of noisy kids for god knows how long, listening to them fight and cry and sing, "I know a song that gets on everybody's nerves." The driver would want to leave just to get away from them. I'm surprised he tried to fix the bus instead of just making a run for it.

But that's the kind of thing you get a Darwin Award for. Driving into a tree because there's a snake in your car would probably qualify.

My best friend Simpson went on an animal-safari trip with his family once. He said it was awesome. He said you'd have to be an idiot to get out of your car.

Simpson lives two streets over from me, but he's moving in a few days. His dad moved out a long time ago, and his mom just found a new house for them. It's in another subdivision, with its own junior high school. That's a harsh blow, because Simpson has been my best friend since kindergarten. I have a lot of friends, but none as close as him. Even if he sucks at piercing, there's no way I'd let any of my other friends even try to do my eyebrow. His new place is so far away it would take a very long time to bike there. Dad is so wrapped up in his time machine he'll never drive me. So not only will Simpson be gone from my school, he'll be gone from my whole life. That sucks.

At least school will be somewhere to go. I'm bored. If Mom were here, she'd drive us to sports camps and take us on camping weekends. Or she'd come home like it was a normal day, but then after dinner she'd walk into my room and say, "Hey, Josh, I bought you a new game that gets high user ratings." Or she'd finish her work and ask, "Anyone want to play Clue?" which we played for Kit Kat sticks. Sammy always went on Mom's team and gave away half her cards. Dad took it very seriously and hid his checklist under the table while he ticked off weapons. It was fun. Mom was a good person to have in the family because without her, we're all just locked in our rooms trying to drum up strong feelings to write about.

I just heard hysterical mewing, so I peeked into Sammy's room. He snuck into the storage cubby at the back of his closet and found his old baby clothes. He has them spread across his bed and he's putting them on the cats. They don't like it, and it's degrading and everything, but man, they look cute. Cleo is trying to keep her dignity in teddy bear overalls and a bonnet. Charlie is wearing blue velvet pants and a matching jacket. He looks like he's begging to be put out of his misery. I have to get the camera.

It'll be good to start at a new school with teachers who never knew Mom, so they won't ask about her or tell me how sorry they are. I wish we'd move to the subdivision with Simpson, because I'm tired of condolences from our neighbors. I never said two words to any of them in my life, but now they all talk to me. Especially Mr. Smitts next door. He used to snowblow our driveway for no good reason, and he'd bring us DVDs he'd rented that weren't due back yet. He's retired and needs things to do, Mom always said. Now he talks to me every time I see him. On my way to the park, he'll be sitting on his porch and he'll call out, "Josh, you are a good boy! You take good care of your little brother! Your mother in Heaven is proud of you!" On our way back he yells out the exact same thing, like I might not have heard him the first time.

He was at Mom's funeral, so I guess he saw me freak out. That's something I can't explain, even though Dr. Tierney has asked me to explain it. Mom told me once that she wanted to be cremated. Dad hated that thought, and so did Aunt Laura—but I don't know why she was involved in the conversation when I wasn't. A son is more important than a sister. Grandma and Grandpa don't like cremation either. So they all decided to bury Mom, even though she didn't want to be buried.

Something weird happened inside me when the earth hit her coffin. I suddenly felt sure she wanted out. I knew she wasn't alive. That used to happen to people sometimes—everyone thought they were dead but they weren't, so they got buried alive—but that never happens anymore. Machines check your vital signs after you die. And with Mom crashing into a tree at high speed, it was pretty obvious she was dead. But I still wanted to stop them from burying her. So I freaked out.

The worst thing is how much it scared Sammy. He's attached to me like a barnacle, so to see me spaz out at Mom's grave shook him up something awful. I still catch him spying on me sometimes, like I can't be trusted. It must have been embarrassing for Dad. He said no, not at all, it was just sad. Dad can be nice when he's not hiding in the basement.

There were so many people at Mom's funeral I don't even know who was there, so when I pass someone and they smile at me, I wonder if they're remembering how I freaked out on Mom's grave. Karen was there—she's sort of my girlfriend, or at least she used to be. She left the funeral early, but not so early that she missed me jumping on Mom's coffin and trying to scratch it open. God, I can't believe I did that.

In the Muslim religion, you're not allowed to freak out at funerals. No wailing, shrieking, beating your chest, scratching your face, pulling your hair, tearing your clothes, breaking things, swearing or blaming God. I didn't scratch my face or tear my clothes, but I did an awful lot of wailing, and I tried to break the coffin open. It's a good thing I'm not Muslim. They only mourn for three days after someone dies— except widows, who are supposed to mourn for four months and ten days. People probably mourn a lot longer if they loved the dead person, but three days is all that's required. Then it's back to life as usual. If you're Muslim, you believe the dead person is going to their afterlife, and you're not supposed to be sad about that.

It's like how Christians believe in Heaven. There's no set time for mourning in Christian churches. But we're not Christian, either, so it doesn't matter. We're not anything. We don't know what to do.

I should go make dinner now. Dad said he would make it, but that was an hour ago, and nothing's cooking. I do a lot of the work Mom used to do at home. I feed Sammy and do the dishes and laundry. I shrunk every pair of Sam's pajamas by washing them in hot water with his sheets. I don't understand why they make pajamas from cloth that shrinks. When a kid pees the bed every night after his mom dies, it makes sense to wash all the dirty stuff together in hot water. Now Sammy's running around in pajamas that are too small, and it'll be years before Dad gets off his butt to go buy new ones.

Aunt Laura came over yesterday to return a pie plate Mom brought to her house at Easter. She said she'd come back soon and take us pajama shopping. Maybe by then I'll have some strong feelings to write about.

Saturday, August 4ᵗʰ

I'm starting to think maybe Dad put the snake in Mom's car. On purpose. Maybe not to kill her, but to stop her from going out. He was ticked off that she was going to work on a Saturday, because it meant he had to stay home and babysit. That's what he called it when he looked after us—babysitting. Like he was getting paid for it.

The police suspected Dad at first, but they couldn't prove anything. Babysitting isn't much of a motive. And a snake isn't much of a weapon. It's not something you'd see on *America's Most Wanted*. But I think the police didn't dig deep enough. Parents always have secrets they throw at their kids when it's least expected. Like, "Hey, kids, I'm building a time machine to disappear in. Have a nice life." I just know in my gut that he's to blame.

Maybe he thought Mom was going to leave us to be with some other guy. That happened to my friend, Ameer. His father kicked his mother out of the house because she was dating some other guy. He didn't try to kill her, but he yells at her in the mall whenever they cross paths. I saw it once, when Ameer and I were buying soccer shoes. His mom came out of the jewelry store and stopped dead in her tracks. She smiled at Ameer, but then his dad started freaking out so she ran away, clutching her purse and looking terrified. Ameer's dad kept yelling at her even after she'd turned the corner. I didn't understand a word he screamed, because he wasn't speaking English, but everybody in the mall could guess what he meant. Ameer never said a word. He just stared at the wall of sports socks. He hasn't mentioned his mother once since she moved out. I think he's still in shock over the whole thing.

My friend Simpson was totally surprised when his parents divorced. His dad came home from work on a Friday three months ago and said he had big news. Simpson said his mom was excited, like she thought his dad was going to tell them he'd booked a family trip to France. Then his dad announced that he had a girlfriend who was pregnant and he was going to marry her. And that was it. He left. The next day a moving truck showed up. That's the thing that bothered Simpson the most—the truck showing up on Saturday morning. It meant his dad had planned to leave long before he told Simpson and his mom. You just don't know what parents are up to.

Maybe Dad thought Mom was going to leave us to be with some other guy, so he wanted to kill her. A lot of men kill their wives, and I bet it comes as a total surprise to their kids. Some Darwin Award winners are men who tried to kill their wives, but ended up killing themselves because they were too stupid to think of a plan that would work. One guy threw his wife out the window, but she grabbed the power lines and saved herself. Then the guy jumped out the window to try to knock her off. How stupid is that? He crashed into the street, dead. And really, he deserved to die. It's wrong to kill someone, especially your wife. Then you wouldn't have anyone who loves you.

I'm pretty sure Mom loved Dad, because she used to dance with him in the kitchen while she was making soup. That was the only thing she ever cooked: a hundred kinds of soup with cheese biscuits. They were all weird soups, like carrot and orange, or mushroom and black bean, or garlic and squash— nothing Sammy and I would ever eat, though the biscuits were good. If Dad came in to see what Mom was cooking—maybe he was hoping it would be something other than soup—she would put her hand on his shoulder and dance and smile like she loved him so much. So normally he wouldn't try to kill her. But if he thought she wanted to leave him, and that she'd be dancing and smiling with some other guy, then maybe he would. I know she'd never leave me and Sammy—she'd come back for us, even if she had some other guy—but she might have left Dad.

What builds the case against Dad is that Mom's job came with life insurance that gives Dad two years of her salary. Which is one hundred thousand dollars times two, and that's a lot of money. I know this because I've been snooping through the mail. Maybe Dad killed Mom for the money, and also for vengeance because of some other guy.

I used to be sure that Mom and Dad loved each other, but Simpson says you never know for sure. He heard his dad say that he never loved his mom, not even for one second. It's hard to believe you could live with someone for thirteen years and have a kid with them and kiss them goodnight every single day and never love them for one second. But what do I know?

If Mom's death was actually a murder, it wouldn't qualify for a Darwin Award, even if it's a stupid way to be murdered. I checked out the Award requirements.

To win, you have to show an astounding misapplication of judgment. For example, a woman on a bus trip wanted a cigarette, but she wasn't allowed to smoke on the bus, so she jumped out. And since the bus was moving, she astoundingly misapplied her judgment and got crushed under the wheels.

Crashing into a tree is pretty astounding too. But a phobia makes you scared out of your mind, like you truly believe your life is in danger. So Mom doesn't deserve a Darwin Award. She was a university professor and very smart. She should have had even more kids, because she had such good genes. She should have donated her eggs to other people who weren't as smart as she was.

I went and sat in Dad's room for a while, because it feels like Mom's still there. I was snooping a bit, and I looked in her drawers. She had pictures from work tucked away. In one picture she had her arm around a man who looked like he adored her. Maybe she was dating him, and Dad found out. I saw that same guy crying at her funeral. Dad looked at him funny, like he recognized him. Or maybe he suspected him. The guy was crying like he had lost his best friend. He didn't freak out like me—but he had dark skin and hair, so maybe he's Muslim and he tried not to wail and tear his clothes. He was definitely weeping, which you're allowed to do if you're Muslim.

I freaked out again this morning when Aunt Laura came over with groceries and told me everything would be okay. I threw the groceries down and stomped on them. Aunt Laura got mad and left, so I had to scrape a dozen squashed tomatoes off the floor. It was totally gross. I freaked out because I hate the words *Everything will be okay*. Mom's death is not a broken cup we can clean up. I know you can make most things better, even really serious things. If you fail a grade, you can make it up. If you lose your job, you can find another one. If you go to jail, you can do your sentence and get out. But dead is dead. There's no way to make it okay.

Aunt Laura got mad and called me a spoiled brat, which is pretty harsh given the circumstances. She yelled, "You're not the only kid in the world who ever lost a parent!" She's forty years old, and Grandma and Grandpa are healthy as can be, so what does she know?

I was being a brat because I thought I could get away with it. I'd never have stomped the groceries if I thought for a second I'd have to clean them up. I freaked out at Aunt Laura once before, and she let me get away with it. It was two days after the funeral. She came over to cook dinner and said, "Don't worry, Josh. Everything's okay." Obviously it wasn't, because Mom was dead and Dad was talking about building a time machine, and he wasn't joking. I threw the frying pan across the room and started screaming. She didn't say a word that time. She just took a new pan from under the stove and kept slicing vegetables.

In the Jewish religion, the week after the funeral is called *shiva*. That's a totally different Shiva from the Hindu god of destruction. During the Jewish *shiva*, the mourners stay home while people visit them. The visitors aren't supposed to speak unless they're answering a question, so they don't annoy the mourners with stupid small talk. The mourners don't have to ask questions if they don't want to. They can totally ignore the visitors if they feel like it, and the visitors are supposed to just accept that. The mourners aren't supposed to freak out and throw frying pans, but the visitors aren't supposed to say everything's okay, are they? But we're not Jewish, so it doesn't matter.

For me, the first week of mourning was a freakish time warp. Usually I play cards every Saturday at the Dungeon, which is the basement of a gaming shop where they hold *Magic* tournaments. The morning before Mom died, I was at the Dungeon, and I told my friend Pete that my first soccer game was coming up the next day. But Mom died, so of course I didn't go to Sunday's game. I just walked around in a daze.

That's called *aninut* in the Jewish religion, that initial shock of death. It's the first stage of mourning, and it only lasts until the burial. Then *shiva* starts.

It's probably a good thing we're not Jewish because when the next Saturday came, and I'd been walking around the house in a daze all week, Pete called to ask if we could drive him to the Dungeon because it was raining and he didn't want to take his bike. I was about to tell him I couldn't go, but Dad said he would drive us because it would do me good to get out of the house. As soon as we picked up Pete, he asked, "How was the soccer game?" And that's when it hit me that it had only been a week since Mom died. Pete didn't even know she was dead. It was so weird because it felt like a couple of months, but really it had only been four days since the funeral.

I said to Pete, "I didn't actually go to the game, because my mom died." There was silence in the car for a minute, and then Pete said, "Are you serious?" He was looking at me like I was some kind of freak for going out to play cards when my mom just died. I couldn't explain to him about the time warp and how Dad said it would do me good to get out. It didn't do me any good. Every time I spoke to someone, I could feel Pete looking at me weird. Maybe he's Jewish and he thought I should be home ignoring my visitors for *shiva*.

Sammy just came into my room to watch *Scooby-Doo*. He has a DVD of his favorite episode with the band Simple Plan. We just rented it from Blockbuster, and he watched it for three hours straight in the living room. Dad probably told him to go do something else, so he brought it up here to watch.

We also rented some *Power Ranger* DVDs because Mom and Sammy used to get up at 6:30 on Sunday mornings to watch *Power Rangers* together. Sam found an old series at Blockbuster called *Mystic Force*. He says he's getting up early to watch it tomorrow. Maybe I'll get up with him to make sure he doesn't wander off. Sammy talks to Mom pretty much constantly—and obviously she isn't really there—so for all we know, she'll tell him to wander off one day, and he'll just go.

He wandered into a cow field during my soccer game last night. I missed all the July games, but the coach called yesterday to ask me to play again. I'm the top scorer in the league, and they'll lose without me. The coach didn't say that though. He said it would help me take my mind off things. I'm guessing Simpson's mom talked to the coach about how I'm spending the summer mourning in my pajamas, like an extended *aninut* shock period, and she told him to call me. I can't see calling somebody whose mom just died and asking them to play soccer unless another mom told you it was a good idea.

When I'm playing soccer, it's like there's nothing else in the world. It's truly awesome. Hardly anything feels like that anymore. Sammy says he wants to play too. Since the season is half over and sign-up was in April, I don't think they'll let him join. But I'll ask the coach about it. Sammy could use something to take his mind off things too.

We won our game. I scored twice. Dad read a book the whole time—that's why Sammy wandered into the cow field. I had to go get him and remind Dad to keep an eye on him. Other than that, it was a great game. I was surprised that Dad drove me. For most games I'll get a ride with Simpson's mom, but he's with his father this weekend, and I didn't want to ask.

On the way to the game, Sammy was afraid to get in the car. It was the first time he'd been in one since the funeral, and he totally freaked out.

Dad told him the car didn't kill Mom, but a snake in the car scared her so much that she crashed. I tried very hard to explain how it wasn't the snake but Mom's fear of the snake that killed her. Sammy didn't get it. Now he thinks snakes are evil. This is a real drag because he used to like snakes and now he wants to kill them.

Sam asked, "How did the snake get in Mom's car?" I had no answer for that. I didn't say that maybe Dad put it there on purpose. First, I'm not sure it was Dad, and second, Dad was standing there listening. So I lied and said the snake climbed in when Mom left the trunk open.

Sam finally got in the car, but only after we searched it for snakes for twenty minutes. He spent the whole ride talking to Mom in a small whispery voice. He looked left to ask a question and then he looked right to answer it. That was definitely weird. But he didn't freak out once we got going, and we were only ten minutes late, so it turned out all right.

The thing about having *Scooby-Doo* on the TV five inches from your face is that it's nearly impossible not to watch it. Even though I've seen this episode fifty times, my eyes are glued to it and I'm almost interested. Sammy's talking along with the characters in each of their voices. He knows every single line. He never stutters when he puts on voices. When he speaks on his own, he takes five minutes to get a sentence out. But talking along with the TV, he's as fast as anyone else. So it's not his ability to say words that's the problem. It's something else, something that gets between his thoughts and his words. Man, everything about people is so complicated.

Sunday, August 5th

I think it was either Dad or the crying guy who put the snake in Mom's car. Maybe that's why the guy cried so much at her funeral, because he was sorry he'd killed her. Maybe he put the snake in her car to scare her so she wouldn't drive. Maybe he's worried about global warming and he wants people to walk. It wasn't a fuel-efficient car. It was more of a gas-guzzler.

I wrote the Darwin Society and asked them not to nominate Mom for an award. I wrote out a list of smart things she did, and I mentioned that she'd already had kids, so it was too late for natural selection. But they don't care about that. You can get a Darwin Award if you're eighty and you've totally polluted the species with your stupid genes.

Most people who've won Darwin Awards did way stupider things than Mom. For example, a guy in Australia put a firecracker between his butt cheeks, and it blasted apart his pelvis. He lived, but he can't have kids, so he won a Darwin Award. That's a horrible thing to happen to someone, but it was also astoundingly stupid.

A lot of people who win Darwin Awards are drunk when they do the stupid thing that kills them. You're eligible for an Award if you're drunk, but not if you're insane. I don't know where phobic fits in. I'm waiting to hear back.

School information came in the mail today. It actually came on Friday but for some reason it was delivered to Mr. Smitts next door, and he just dropped it off this morning. I find that suspicious. He probably saw the package in our mailbox and thought it was something worth stealing, like the *Medieval II: Total War* game I ordered six weeks ago from California.

A big package came for Sammy, because this will be his first year of school. He's going to a French immersion school where they have kindergarten all day, every day, just like a regular grade. It's a good thing they had registration back in February when Mom was alive, because if Dad had to do it now, it just wouldn't happen. He opened the school package and sighed. He didn't even read it. I handed him our lists of school supplies, and he smiled like it's already taken care of, when of course it's not.

When Mr. Smitts came over with the mail, he also brought Pillsbury chocolate-chip cookies, and they were still warm. I was surprised, because he doesn't seem like a baker. Even though you just have to spoon the dough onto a cookie sheet, that would be a big effort for someone like Mr. Smitts. I offered him a cookie, and we all sat on the porch and had milk and cookies—me and Sammy and Mr. Smitts. Dad was in the basement. He came up for two seconds to say hello, but he didn't even eat a cookie. I thought that was rude. If somebody goes to the trouble of making you cookies, you should eat one.

It was nice visiting with Mr. Smitts, except he went on and on about Mom until it started to bug me. He spoke of her in the present tense, and I found that disturbing. Sammy was thrilled, of course. He finally found someone else who thinks Mom is still alive.

After Mr. Smitts left, I gave Sam the same talk Mom gave me every year before school started, about how privileged we are to live in a country where all children go to school. Even though it can feel like a prison, going to school is something kids all over the world would love to do if they could. You learn to read and write and understand geography and mathematics so that you can grow up and work instead of starve. I told Sammy that by going to school he could become an archaeologist or a game designer or a doctor or a poet or the mayor or whatever. Mom said poets don't make much money, but doctors and mayors do.

Sammy didn't need the talk, because he's bored out of his skull this summer. He's dying to go to school just to get out of the house. Even if he had to starve afterward, he'd still go.

We talked a bit about growing up and how I want to become a game designer. I've been planning a computer game called *Evolution* where you start out as a single cell, and you're in competition with other cells, and you have to choose different DNA components to make you the fittest for your environment. Then the environment changes, and whole groups of cells die off while others thrive. If you live, you evolve into a multicellular animal—or you could be a plant, but who'd want to? The different species change the environment, and the environment changes the species, so it's very exciting. You evolve into a fish, then an amphibian and a reptile, and ultimately a primate. If you become *Homo sapiens sapiens*, you win the game. Most people think if you got to be any old *Homo sapiens* you'd win. But no. *Homo sapiens idaltu* went extinct, so you wouldn't want to be them. All the species in the game are real species that went extinct, but some of them were the ancestors of today's species and others were dead ends. When you choose your DNA, you won't know which one you are. It's going to be an awesome game.

Last summer I went to computer camp with Ameer, and we learned how to make very simple games. I wanted to go again this summer, but Dad either cancelled or forgot, because I haven't gone anywhere since Mom died. I probably wouldn't get to another soccer game if Simpson's parents didn't drive me.

Most of the kids I know want to be game designers too, so the competition will be fierce. That's kind of like my game. I don't know yet if I have the right DNA to make it to the top.

Everyone says you can be what you want or get what you want if you just try hard enough, but that's not true. There are kids all over the world who want to go to school, but they can't because there's no school where they live or no money for teachers. Other kids go to school, but they can't pass because they're just not smart. Trying hard isn't going to make them rocket scientists. Some kids might want to play soccer or piano, but they can't because they're paralyzed. It's not going to happen no matter how much they believe in their dream.

And there are kids whose mothers die slowly of cancer. For years they really want their moms to live, and the moms really want to live, and the whole family tries to make it happen, but it doesn't. The moms die anyway. Sometimes you can't be something or have something no matter how much you want it and no matter how hard you try. Some things you just have to suffer through.

That's what I think of when I see a cross, like they have in Christian churches, with Jesus on it. When you're not a Christian, it's a horrible thing to see a cross like that, with Jesus hanging there dying. For Christians, it reminds them that God suffered for them. But it reminds me that things don't happen just because you want them to. I think of all the people who loved Jesus and thought he was God. I picture them standing there watching him die and feeling just absolutely positive that God would take him down from the cross any second now to prove that he was God. But that didn't happen.

Everyone who believes in God must feel like that sometimes. They must feel absolutely sure that God is going to do something any second now to make things right. Like all those Jewish people who were killed by the Nazis. They believed in God. They must have wished for God to save them. If you were standing in a big group of people, with your family next to you, and Nazi soldiers started shooting everyone in the group—so you knew they were going to shoot you too—if you really believed in God, you would wait for Him to save you and your family. But it didn't happen. God didn't save anyone. Millions of people were killed. Millions of people wishing as hard as anybody ever wished anything.

I don't believe in God. My expectations are low.

In the Jewish religion, the time of mourning keeps going after the seven days of *shiva* are over. The next period is called *shloshim*. It lasts thirty days from the burial, so it includes the ignoring-people period. You're not allowed to get married or go to parties during *shloshim*, and men don't shave or get haircuts. I told that to Dad, and he said, "Okay, Josh, we won't shave or get haircuts." Then I told him *shloshim* ended for us two days ago, and he got sad because he's been shaving. I said it was okay because we're not Jewish. He smiled and went to work on his time machine.

I wish we were Jewish because they're so organized about what to do after somebody dies, whereas we're dragging ourselves around feeling like we should just write in our journals and let the garbage pile up. I would like a list of things I'm not supposed to do, so that I'd know if it's okay to go to my soccer games and punch the air when I score. I don't think the Jewish religion mentions soccer in particular, but since they have a list of stuff to avoid during *shloshim*, whatever's not on the list would be okay to do.

After *shloshim*, the rest of the year until the anniversary of the person's death is called *shneim asar chodesh*. It's still a time of mourning, but most of life goes back to normal. You're not supposed to go to parties, and you're supposed to say prayers for the dead person. So if I were Jewish, I'd know for sure that I could go to soccer now. But I'm not, so it sucks.

For example, tomorrow is a civic holiday and Dad has the day off work. If we were Jewish, we could go bowling or to a movie or something, so long as it wasn't a party. I asked Dad what we were doing for the holiday, and he said, "Josh, we're in mourning." That means he's spending the holiday in the basement. I reminded him that he sent me out to play cards when it was still *shiva*, but he just shrugged.

I called Simpson, and he invited me to meet him at the beach tomorrow. That's where his dad is passing him back to his mom for the week. I asked if I could bring Sammy, and he said that would be great. Simpson's mom loves Sammy. She bites her finger like it's just too cute when he says "hostable" instead of "hospital," or "liberry" instead of "library," or—my personal favorite— "really-ized" instead of "realized." It's hard not to like Sam, because he's four and a half and totally cute, and when Mom wasn't dead, he was always happy.

I asked Dad if he'd drive us to the beach to meet Simpson, and he said okay. A long drawn-out

"Okaaaayyy." That means he'll forget to pick us up.
I put our bikes in the trunk so we can bike home after
swimming. It takes Sammy an hour to ride the bike
path from the beach, but that's better than waiting
for Dad not to show up, then hitchhiking and being
taken hostage by some sicko guy who picks up hitch-
hikers just to torture them.

So now we have something fun to do tomorrow
that isn't a party.

We won both soccer games this weekend, Friday
and Saturday. I scored seven goals altogether. I was
truly awesome. Simpson scored twice, and his dad
took us out for ice cream. I don't like his dad as much
as his mom. He hardly talks to me, and he looks at
me weird. Dad says that's because he feels guilty about
leaving Simpson's mother. Whatever. He bought me
a Blizzard at Dairy Queen. I couldn't finish it, so I
brought half home for Sammy, and he really appre-
ciated that. He'd wanted to come to the game, but
Simpson's dad is not the sort of person you ask to
watch Sammy at a soccer game. He's one of those dads
who yell "Put your glasses on!" at the referee every
five minutes. He wouldn't care if Sammy wandered
into the cow field. When Simpson told his dad that
Sammy talks to Mom as if she's alive, his dad said,
"That's just crazy." So Sammy didn't come to my game.
But he liked the ice cream.

I asked my coach if Sam could join soccer even though it's almost over. He asked what year Sammy was born. If he'd just turned four this year, he couldn't play. But since his birthday is in October, he can play with the five-year-olds. My coach told me that the coach of five-year-old soccer lives on our street, and I think I know which house. There's a guy across the street and two doors down who plays soccer with his kid on their front lawn. I'll ask him tomorrow if Sammy can join his team. I'll get Sam to come with me and look really cute and pathetic but also really good at soccer.

This will be difficult, because Sam has developed a new habit of walking backward everywhere he goes. He says he wants to see people as he leaves them so that if they die, he'll remember their faces. This is a weird new habit on top of his other weird habits.

He says he remembers Mom's back the day she died. She was wearing her pretty red dress with tiny yellow flowers. He remembers her bare arms, and the way her purse swung off her shoulder into the crook of her elbow. She laughed and turned her head a little so he saw the tiniest bit of her cheek and nose, just enough to tell she was smiling as she left the house. He remembers her hair bouncing on her shoulders. She'd just brushed it, and it was shiny. But he can't remember her face. If she'd been walking backward, the last thing he'd have seen would have been her smile, and that's what he would like to remember. So he wants everyone to walk backward. That's the only way he'll walk now, which will make it hard for him to be really good at soccer.

This makes me think that if Mom was wearing a pretty dress and she'd just brushed her hair, maybe she was going on a date with the crying Muslim guy who adored her. So maybe it was Dad who put the snake in her car, after all. Maybe he thought she'd hop in the car, see the snake and hop back out. Even though Mom wasn't religious, she did say, "That's a sign," an awful lot, like she thought there was a spy network of angels passing notes and codes. If she'd seen a snake in her car, she'd have taken it as a sign to stay home.

Maybe Dad put the snake right on her seat but it hid underneath and only came out later. It takes about ten minutes to get to the highway, and Mom would have freaked out the very first second she saw it. Maybe Dad just meant to scare her, but he killed her by accident, and that's why he's gone insane.

He should have known the snake would kill her. She used to freak out at toy snakes, even when she knew they were plastic. She'd freak out at something on the floor that was just in the shape of a snake, like a sock or a belt. Dad would have to be a total idiot to put a snake in her car. Which doesn't rule him out.

Maybe the snake had been hiding in the car for a long time. Someone at her work might have put it there on Friday, and it hid under the seat until Saturday. Maybe someone was trying to kill her and the crying guy together. If he's married or something, his wife might have done it. Really, we're lucky we weren't all in the car when the snake came out of hiding.

It's good that Mom went off the road into a tree instead of hitting other cars and killing people. She would have felt terrible about that. It took the police a while to figure out what had gone wrong. First they thought it was a mechanical failure. Then they found the snake and thought Mom had a heart attack. But Dad knew right away that Mom must have freaked out, so he told them about her phobia.

After that, the police interviewed me and Sammy four times about what Dad was doing before Mom left the house, and whether Mom and Dad had been fighting lately. But then they ruled it an accident. They don't know where the snake came from. Maybe it was in a bag someone put in the backseat. Or maybe one of the cats carried it to the car. Except our cats hate going in the car, and how could you not notice a snake in your bag? Maybe it had lived in the car ever since Mom bought it.

There could be other things waiting to kill you. Things you'd never think about, like a snake in a car or a tree about to fall down. Anything could kill you at any time. Maybe Sammy is right about walking backward. Except it's dangerous. Not because he'll walk into a car—he's actually very skilled at walking backward—but because our neighbors will see him walking backward in shrunken pajamas talking to his dead mother, and they'll call the police to take him to another home where he'll be properly parented. I'll be left alone with Dad, and I'll go nuts. And then the whole family will be officially insane.

I told Sammy it was okay to walk backward if he's with me, but only for now while we're in our time of mourning. And he said, "No, it's afternoon." That cracked me up.

He walked backward the whole way to the park yesterday. I waved at the neighbors to reassure them that he was properly supervised. Karen's mom was sitting on her porch smoking. She asked how we were doing. I guess she was at the funeral, but I don't remember because there were so many people. Karen was there, so of course her mom would have been there.

I wish Karen was here right now, so I'd know for sure if she's my girlfriend. She's at camp for the summer, one of those camps where you live in a cabin with a group of strangers who become your best friends in a week. I don't have a clue if she's my girlfriend or not.

Sammy told Karen's mom that Mom was killed by a giant snake and that he doesn't like snakes anymore. Karen's mom said she never liked snakes either.

She said I should write to Karen at camp. She went inside and came back out with an address. Her cigarette smoke blew in my eyes when she passed it to me.

Sammy told her that smoking was bad for her, but she just laughed like she was going to live forever.

Wednesday, August 8th

I think it was either Dad, the crying guy or a nutty student who put the snake in Mom's car. I don't think garter snakes climb into shopping bags or get caught by cats. But crazy killers are everywhere.

I looked up snakes online. There's actually a whole genus of garter snakes called *Thamnophis*, with a dozen different species. The one that killed Mom was a "common garter snake." That's a stupid name for a species. It should be called the dog-fearing garter snake or the path-finding garter snake or something halfway interesting.

Common garter snakes are about two feet long and harmless—unless you have a phobia and one slithers out from under your seat while you're driving on the highway, in which case they're deadly.

The interesting thing about them is that people keep them as pets. They grab them while they're hibernating and put them in terrariums. So anybody could have kept one as a pet and tossed it in Mom's car when the opportunity arose.

Another interesting thing is they discharge a bad-smelling secretion from their anal gland if you try to pick them up. That's a nasty but effective defense strategy. I'd drop any snake that pooped on me, for sure.

I also looked up stalkers online, because they're the sort of people who might find out you have a phobia and then put a snake in your car. I read that universities are especially full of stalkers.

I went to the university and had a look around, but I couldn't tell who was a stalker and who wasn't. I stopped at Mom's office and met the crying guy from her funeral. He was right there in her office—not stalking but working. It's his office now. He's an associate professor, like Mom was. His name is Professor Mitchell Johnston.

Johnston doesn't sound like a Muslim name, and that's because the guy's not Muslim. So he could have bewailed and torn his clothes and jumped on the coffin with me at Mom's funeral and it wouldn't have been against his religion. He's not Jewish either. I asked. He's Roman Catholic, which is the Christian religion with the pope. I've been to Mom's work a few times, and I never saw the guy before in my life until the funeral. But he must have worked there a while. He had a photograph of Mom on the wall—it showed the two of them sitting together smiling. He probably had his eye on her office for years.

There were two boxes of Mom's stuff in the corner of the room. The crying guy said he'd been meaning to drop them off at our house, since nobody came to pick them up. I think he was too scared of meeting Dad to come by, either because he killed Mom, or he thinks Dad killed her, or one of his nutty jealous students killed her.

Two students came into the office while I was there. They were totally crazy and could easily have been stalkers. They went on and on about Mom like they knew everything about her. The girl hugged me so hard it was disturbing. I'd never met her before in my life, and she was holding me and crying, which is the sort of thing a stalker would do. Her name was something like "Cheetah." It was an Indian name and she had a strong accent, so I had no idea what name she said, but four times was enough to ask her to repeat it. Her boyfriend's name was Jim. He was attached to her practically like a Siamese twin.

Cheetah is getting her PhD in medieval poetry. Mom was her thesis advisor. Jim tagged along on their meetings. Mom told them a lot about me. You never think of people you love talking about you to total strangers.

For example, Dad goes to work every day and he never packs a lunch, so he probably goes out with people from work. It would be strange, even for Dad, to just sit there eating in total silence, so he probably tells people things about me and Sammy. I bet he doesn't say anything at all about his time machine though, or they'd have fired him by now.

The nutty students stayed a long time in Mom's old office, but when I started to open a box of her stuff, the crying guy shouted, "I'll take those home for you!" and shoved everybody out the door. Like he just couldn't bear to look at Mom's coffee cup. He put the boxes in the backseat of his car and put my bike in the trunk. It's a long ride from campus, and I was pretty much overjoyed to get a ride home.

The crying guy carried Mom's boxes to the porch, but when Aunt Laura stepped outside and gave him the evil eye, he left in a hurry. Aunt Laura had been watching Sammy all afternoon. She was fed up with his walking backward, and she looked about a hundred years old.

I made the mistake of peeking in Sammy's journal. I thought it would be blank, but it was half-full already. It contains forty-two drawings of killer cars being smacked by trees. Sam's cars have eyes and teeth and sometimes a person squashed inside them, bloody and dead. Fortunately, Sammy's not a very good artist, so if a total stranger found his book, they'd think it was abstract art.

After the forty-two killer-car drawings, there are sixteen drawings of scary snakes with enormous fangs striking a person who is bloody and dead. We have a family meeting with Dr. Tierney soon, and I think we should bring our journals. Sammy can't start kindergarten walking backward and drawing killer snakes. He'll be the weird kid right from day one. That's the kind of hole you never dig yourself out of. There's a kid in my school named Aaron who used to pick his nose and eat his boogers all through kindergarten. He's twelve now, but I still think of him as the kid who ate his green slimers. In gym class no one wants him on the team because he'll pass the ball with the hands that went from his nose to his mouth all those years ago.

Dr. Tierney needs to get Sammy on a different path. He needs to give Sam guidelines for working with a journal. I also wish he'd give us guidelines for mourning Mom. Without religion, you're just left hanging.

Cheetah the stalker-student was very surprised that I knew about the Hindu religion, which has a mourning period of thirteen days after someone dies.

During that time, you cover up the pictures in your house, you don't visit temples, and you don't serve food or drinks to guests. But you don't ignore them either. You wear white, which is the Hindu color of mourning, and you bathe twice a day. Cheetah said you can mourn longer than thirteen days, but that could annoy the dead person, who's about to be reincarnated.

I might wash my white T-shirts to wear in respect of Mom, even though we're not Hindu and it's already been forty days. I think Mom would like a good, hard grieving. She'd have been disappointed if we'd stopped mourning thirteen days after she died.

In some religions, you put up a shelf for the dead and keep it forever. You light a special candle on holidays to include the dead person's memory in your celebrations. I think Mom would want a shelf like that. She wouldn't want to be forgotten, even if she was reincarnated, which I don't believe in. Mom kept a picture of her dog Kiwi on the fridge, and he died before I was born. That's a clue that thirteen days isn't long enough for her. But then she got Charlie and Cleo, our cats, so who knows? Maybe if we keep Mom's picture up, she'd be happy even if we get a whole new mom some day.

I know she would want us to be happy, not crying and walking backward and tinkering with the space-time continuum. If she saw us at this exact moment—Dad in the basement denying reality, Sam in his room drawing psycho snakes, and me here griping—she'd just shake her head. Actually, she'd probably tell us all to go to bed because it's midnight.

Sammy has lost all concept of a bedtime. Mom used to have strict rules for him. She gave fifteen-, ten- and five-minute warnings, followed by a bath at seven-thirty, a snack while Sam's hair dried at eight— either cereal or toast, no exceptions—then two stories in bed and lights out. Now Dad comes upstairs at eight o'clock to use the bathroom and make a cup of tea and he says, "Gee, Sammy, it's getting late. I think you should go to bed." Then he goes back to the basement and comes up again at ten and says the exact same thing.

I read Sammy an old Superman comic at bedtime tonight, where Superman gets trapped in Hell and has to trick the devil and escape. Unfortunately, devils are among the bazillion things Sammy's afraid of, so he was crying by page three. I made up a *Scooby-Doo* ending where the devil isn't really the devil. He's a professor who built a pretend Hell as part of an elaborate plan to steal Superman's money. Sammy was very happy with that ending. Not that it helped him get to sleep.

He's still awake two hours later, drawing with spy-glasses on. Simpson came over tonight and brought his old spyglasses for Sammy. They have a mirror at the side that lets you see what's behind you, so Sam is less likely to walk backward into a car. It would be better if he'd walk forward, but at least he won't get killed. Now he won't take the glasses off. "Safety first," he says.

A weird thing happened when Simpson was over. We were playing *Shadow of Rome* in my room with the door closed—Sammy's not allowed to watch that game, because you can rip off a guy's arm and beat him to death with it, and Sam has enough problems already. Simpson said out of the blue, "I sent Karen a letter at camp to tell her how we're doing."

That disturbed me. Simpson knows I've liked Karen forever, and he saw us kissing at graduation, so what's he doing writing to her at camp? Nobody writes to a girl unless he's her boyfriend.

I was thinking how much I'm going to miss Simpson when he moves, but maybe the upside is that once he's in a different school, he won't try to steal my girlfriend behind my back while I'm in mourning. Anyway, I have a lot of other friends.

Yesterday at the park, Simpson and I played basketball with Turner and Ameer. It was great. I hadn't seen them since school ended. Ameer talked about everything I'd missed at computer camp. That bugged me, but basketball was fun. I took Sammy with us, and he played in the sandbox next to the court.

It got a bit weird, because the four-year-old bully was there—Darren from down the street—and he threw a bucket of sand at Sammy's face. Like the whole bucket, not just the sand inside it. Sammy got a big red welt on his forehead, and he started to cry. Darren got ready to bash him with the bucket again. Seriously, there is something wrong with that kid. He was laughing like a maniac and getting his bucket ready to swing. Ameer beaned him with the basketball. He got him right in the head, and it was a hard shot. It's a good thing he didn't break the kid's nose, or we'd have been in trouble. It hit him in back of the head and didn't break anything, but it shut him up pretty fast. He stumbled a little and dropped his bucket on his own foot, which made Sammy laugh right through his tears.

We all cheered, the four of us grade sevens. We cheered like it was the greatest thing in the world to hit a little four-year-old kid in the head with a basketball. We gave each other high fives. When I went to pick up the ball, I gave Darren an evil look and held up the basketball as if I might smash him with it. And my friends laughed. Crazy.

The kid's mother didn't say a word, which made me think of Mom. If Mom had seen us do that, oh my god, she'd have had an awful lot to say.

Friday, August 10ᵗʰ

I did the laundry and turned all the white stuff gray, so now I'm wearing a grubby blotched T-shirt in memory of Mom. It's a good thing we're not Hindu.

Why do they make clothes out of material that shrinks or leaks color? We're supposed to be a technologically advanced society. Our washing machine has a computer inside it. You'd think I could toss in a pair of pajamas and a T-shirt and they'd come out the same size and color as before, only clean. But no. They come out shrunken and gray.

I'm tired of doing housework. When Mom was alive, we had a maid who came every Monday and cleaned the house and changed the beds and did the laundry. But the Monday after Mom died, Grandma sent the maid away and changed the beds herself.

Grandma and Grandpa went back to British Columbia after the funeral. I tried to get the maid back a few weeks ago, but she took one look around and said we needed a spring-cleaning team. And it's not even spring.

If there was a stupid, dangerous machine to clean houses, I would use it right now and probably get electrocuted and win a Darwin Award.

I looked at some crime websites yesterday. There are a lot of insane people out there who kill people for no good reason. It could be anyone who put the snake in Mom's car. Maybe Mom gave Cheetah a bad mark—that's enough reason to kill someone if you're insane. Or maybe the crying guy wanted Mom's office—who knows? I wish I didn't care so much. Unless it was Dad who killed her, what difference does it make how she died? I just wish it never happened.

It sounds spoiled, but I miss Mom's usefulness. She organized my whole life. Since she's been dead, there's nothing going on. I never hear from my friends, and the house is so crazy I don't even want them over. I could tell the other night that Simpson was happy to leave. He said he doesn't want to come over tonight after the game, and I don't blame him. Sammy's always speaking to our dead mother, Dad's a big idiot and I have nothing to talk about except their insanity.

I need to find out if Mom registered me for any camps in late August. I need to be with other people. I played *Civilization* for seven hours straight today— I pretty much conquered the planet. Then I read Sammy a book where Scooby-Doo goes to ancient Rome, until I got a headache and yelled at him and made him cry. And that was my whole day.

I wrote to Karen, but I couldn't think of much to say. I hope she writes back. I've liked her since grade two, and things just got started at graduation when we kissed and she said she really liked me. Then Mom died and Karen went away to camp. Things were really good before Mom died. I know it's not her fault, but why couldn't she have just pulled over?

This is later the same day. Any normal kid my age is sleeping.

We lost our soccer game tonight. I didn't score a single goal, and everyone was mad at me. But why should I have to score every game? Someone else should score for a change.

Simpson's mom applied for a cross-boundary transfer so he can go to the same junior high school as me. That would be good. He said he was switching parents at the game, which is why he couldn't come over tonight. I saw his dad sitting in the bleachers far away from his mom, so I think it's true. Anyway, I had some fun with him at soccer. I teased him because he wore his hat offside, trying to cover up a big scabby thing at the top of his ear. He denies it's a failed and festering attempt at piercing, but what else could it be?

Sammy's in here talking about kindergarten, even though it's past midnight. He was scared in his own room. He says Mom is coming home soon, and he'll sleep in his bed again when she's with him. What am I supposed to say to that?

His journal is almost full. I told him to draw nice things that Mom would like. "Like Power Rangers?" he asked. Only he said it, "Li-i-ike, like, um, uh, uh, like, li-i-i-ike Power Rangers?" He's not like normal stutterers, who can't get their consonants out. Sammy stutters vowels. He fills space with whining gibberish like he's mentally retarded, but really he's not at all. He's really very smart.

I said, "Yeah, like Power Rangers. And flowers and cats and walks in the woods." He said, "And, and, a-a-and treasure hunts a-a-a-and mazes?" I said, "Sure." Then he said, "And, and, a-a-and that will make Mom come home?" I said, "No." So he's probably drawing a psycho snake picture.

Okay. Just now I said to him, "Maybe Mom can see you wherever she is, and she wants to see you draw something she'd like, not a snake that would scare her." That made a strong impression on Sammy. He put down his journal and cried his little eyes out, stuttering, "I'm sorry, Mommy. I-I-I'm sorry I scared you." Little kids cry so hard they break your heart.

He ran to his room and came back with a toy Power Ranger. It's a girl Ranger, a light blue one that he never played with before in his life. Mom used it when they played Power Rangers together. Mom would draw a map on the walkway, like a crazy hopscotch, and she'd put bad guys and wild animals in the squares. Then the Power Rangers would travel the map fighting the bad guys until they saved the world.

Mom said she and I used to play that game too, and we watched *Power Rangers* on TV together when I was little and it came on at a decent time instead of 6:30 Sunday morning. I don't remember ever watching *Power Rangers*. I remember a few things from when I was Sammy's age, but not much. I don't remember starting school.

Mom made a kindergarten book for me, to hold the drawings and crafts I made. It has my class picture in it, but I don't remember any of the kids. I can recognize Simpson, but I don't remember playing with him back then. Mom has stories in the book about things I said and shows I watched and places I went. We went to England that year and I saw Stonehenge and Windsor Castle and all kinds of cool things I don't remember at all.

That means Sammy won't remember Mom by the time he's twelve. And maybe I won't remember her by the time I'm twenty. This is the saddest thought I've had since she died—and I've had a lot of sad thoughts.

Mom and I were really close. She'd tell me nice things about myself, and she'd make my favorite peanut-butter cookies on Sunday even though no one else likes them, and she'd take me to the IMAX whenever a new show came to town. She'd tell me funny jokes and ask if I'd heard any good ones lately. And sometimes I would make her laugh so hard that I could see her fillings and she'd smack the table and cackle like a witch. It was a great feeling to make her laugh like that.

If I forget all that, it will be like it never happened. And even though one day we'll all be dead, and even the earth and the sun will be dead, it just seems wrong to forget Mom while I'm alive and she's not.

Sammy won't remember anything she did for him—the songs she made up and the games she played and the stories she read, and all the good things she brought into his life that are gone now. He'll have an empty hole where Mom should be. And even if she's dead, there should be something there besides a hole.

I'm going to make a scrapbook about Mom, like she did about me in kindergarten. Sammy and I can keep it forever, like a memory shelf, except it's a book.

I just realized that when Sammy ran to his room to get the blue Power Ranger, he ran forward, not backward. So there's hope for him yet. I forgot to ask our neighbor about the five-year-old soccer team, but I'll try to remember before my game tomorrow.

I'm in a better mood now and it's really late, so I should go to bed. Sammy's head is hanging down near his journal and he's drooling on it, so he must be asleep. He looks totally cute and peaceful, and you'd never know he was bawling his eyes out ten minutes ago.

Tuesday, August 14th

We saw Dr. Tierney today, and he didn't ask to see our journals, not even to make sure we've been using them. When I told him about Dad's time machine and Sammy's psycho snakes, he said, "Let's talk about you, Josh." But when I told him that Sammy and I are collecting stories and photographs to make into a scrapbook about Mom, he scrunched his eyebrows together and frowned like that was a completely insane and puzzling idea.

So that confirms my poor opinion of psychiatrists. Except he gave us more journals, and they're probably expensive. So that's good.

Sammy loves the Mommy Book, which is what he calls our scrapbook. We haven't even written it, but in his mind it's already done. We started collecting pictures for it and planning which stories to include. Sam mentioned some of the less nice things about Mom, like how she yelled at me to stop combing my hair and get outside to the bus stop every morning last year. It must be a strong memory for Sam, because he asked about five thousand times, "Are, are, a-a-are we going to have a picture uh-uh-uh-of Mommy screaming at you in the morning?"

I can't decide whether to include mean things like that or just leave them out. Maybe I can make them into funny jokes about life with Mom. But they were never funny at the time.

Man, she hated it when I was late for school. She'd go on and on about how we have a bus system so she shouldn't have to drive me. She'd say, "What if we didn't have a car?" and all sorts of irrelevant things like that. I only missed the bus twice in the whole year, but she yelled at me every single day to get out and wait for it. It's only partly true that I combed my hair slowly on purpose to bug her. I couldn't believe how easy it was to make her mad over something so stupid. She never got mad at other stuff, like when I lost my shoes or forgot my homework. But man, she got mad over the school bus.

At least she got me on the bus, which is more than I expect from Dad. I can see him driving off to work, waving at me in the window while I stay home gaming all day.

He took me to soccer on Saturday though. I scored three goals and we won the game. Sammy cheered, partly in his own voice and partly in his Power Ranger girly voice. It was very embarrassing to Dad, who stared at Sam like he was somebody else's weird kid. Sammy told Dad he wants to play too, because Mom liked soccer. When Dad said it was too late to join, I told him that our neighbor is the five-year-old soccer coach. Dad said, "No way, Josh. They'd never let a five-year-old be coach." I think he was actually making a joke, even though his expression didn't change. That has to be a good sign.

Cheetah dropped by with some photographs this morning. Some happy pictures of Mom at work made me smile and then cry a bit. Cheetah hugged me and cried too. She was soft and warm, and it was nice to hug her.

Her name is actually Chaitan. She wrote it on a photograph of her and Mom. I think that's a weird name because it's a lot like *Sheitan*, which is Persian for Satan. Maybe she's the devil, and she put the snake in Mom's car. Except I don't believe in devils. And she doesn't seem like a devil. She's awfully pretty. When I told her I'd thought her name was Cheetah, she said that was a good name and if she were African she'd want that name. So that's what I'm calling her.

I told her that Ashanti families in Africa mourn people for forty days after the funeral. She said it was cool to know stuff like that, but when I asked her if I was a know-it-all, she said no. That's good, because a lot of know-it-alls win Darwin Awards.

Cheetah already knew about the Darwin Awards. She said she told Mom about them a few years ago. I guess she's been working on her PhD for a long time. When I asked her if she knew how the snake got in Mom's car, she said no. But she looked guilty, so it's hard to say. Maybe she was feeling guilty for liking the Darwin Awards—she started to cry when I said I hoped Mom wouldn't get one. I told her not to cry, because some of them are funny, and it's okay to laugh at the ones that were astoundingly stupid.

I don't think Cheetah put the snake in Mom's car. She was very nice to bring the photographs and let me call her Cheetah. When Sammy walked into the room backward and I explained why he did that, she told him it was an excellent idea. She even left our house walking backward. But since she was crying, if she dies, the last thing we'll remember of her is her face all screwed up and weeping.

It's hard to think that someone you just saw this morning might have died at lunchtime and you wouldn't even know it. With Mom, there was a long time when I was bumming around at home thinking she was at work, but really she was dead. You have no way of knowing. You could say good-bye to your friend on the phone, then remember some joke he made, and think, "He's such a funny guy. I'm sure glad he's my friend." But really he could be dead already. He might have tripped down the stairs and broken his neck.

Mom told the best jokes. She was on a hundred joke e-mail lists—it's hard to see how she got any work done with all those jokes to read. She'd tell me the best ones. On the day she died, she said, "What did the Buddha say to the hot-dog vendor? Make me one with everything." She laughed all bright and happy when she told me that. Sammy didn't get it, of course, but she didn't tell it for him. She told it for me. I know about Buddhism and being one with everything. She told that joke while she was unpacking groceries and putting away the hot dogs. I told it to Simpson later in the day, but he didn't get it either. And by then Mom was already dead. It wasn't right to tell her joke while she was dead. I wish I had known right away.

If there's anybody who's not actually in your line of sight right now, they could be dead. Dad might be sprawled in his time machine, dead of a heart attack. Or a brain attack. Maybe your brain shuts down if you get so stupid it can't stand to live with you. Like if you're building a time machine and ignoring your kids whose mom just died.

I went into the basement to show Dad the pictures Cheetah brought this afternoon, but he must have been out in the yard with Sammy. He has half the basement curtained off. Behind the curtain is a strange rocket-shaped construction covered in a tarp, which I'm guessing is his time machine. I didn't want to look.

Dad's journal was lying on a table behind the curtain. It wasn't full of time-travel theories. It was full of sad thoughts about how much he misses Mom and how he doesn't know if he can go on living and how much he loves me and Sammy. It was frightening to read that he's so sad. I would rather he were just insane.

I don't think Dad put the snake in Mom's car anymore. He wrote that he thinks I did it as a prank. Or maybe he just wrote that to cover his tracks and set me up in case the police start investigating again, and they take his journal as evidence. He should know that I'm not a prankster. Okay, I put fake poop on the porch once. And on April Fools' Day, I wrote a letter saying Dad won a million dollars a year for life. But I would never scare Mom with a snake.

If he reads my journal like I read his, he'll find out it wasn't me.

So I'll say right here that it isn't very nice of him to keep walking forward when Sammy asked him to walk backward. A total stranger did it! But Dad won't do it for his own four-year-old kid who has obviously gone wacko, peeing the bed and speaking to Mom through a Power Ranger. How is Sammy ever going to get through kindergarten without being labeled a freak? It starts in three weeks.

I'd understand if Dad were trying to help Sammy break his walking-backward habit. But Dad's not helping Sammy. He's not even making him supper. We've been eating microwaved hot dogs and Mr. Noodles for five weeks straight. Tonight Sammy clapped when I gave him cinnamon toast. We could use a real dad.

I'm going to accidentally-on-purpose leave this journal on the kitchen counter by the coffeepot so Dad will find it and know for sure that I didn't put the snake in Mom's car. And he can learn that he's failing as a parent.

Thursday, August 16th

Dad was showing no sign of having read my journal, and it was in exactly the same spot where I left it two days ago, so I just went up to him and said, "I didn't put the snake in Mom's car, if that's what you're thinking." He said, "I would never think that, Josh." So obviously he doesn't know that I read his journal. I asked him straight out, "Did you put the snake in Mom's car on purpose so she'd have an accident?" He looked pretty shocked at that. He walked away toward the basement.

I freaked out. I shoved the plant stand over and yelled, "You're a terrible father! You're worse than no parent at all!" Then I started to cry. Sammy ran into the hall, and the girl Power Ranger said she loved me.

Then Cleo came over and started pawing the dirt I'd spilled, like maybe she was going to poop in it. I started laughing hysterically. We're such a pathetic family.

Later, when Dad and I were alone again, he said maybe Sammy put the snake in Mom's car, and that's why he's gone wacko. But I can't see Sammy catching a snake without getting a hundred bites and a lot of bad-smelling anal secretion all over him. The kid can't catch a baseball. I've never tried to catch a snake, but once in the schoolyard I saw Karen grab one right behind its head. She said if you grab a snake anywhere else, it will swing around and bite you. I asked if she'd ever been bitten, and she said, "Yeah, but it doesn't hurt that much." Then she chased me around the schoolyard, laughing.

I wonder why Dad suspected me, since he's seen me run away from snakes. Last fall I lifted up a wooden board behind the shed, and I totally spazzed out when I saw a snake under it. I ran to the deck as if it were chasing me. Meanwhile, Sammy rushed over to check out the snake. If he were older, he'd have shouted, "Josh, my boy, you've discovered a common garter snake!" He loves snakes. He could probably learn to identify all the different species if he took half a minute away from the TV and just looked at a book sometime.

Mom always said she wished she were like Sammy around snakes. If he did manage to catch one, he might have put it in her car, thinking it would help her become unafraid like he was. But it's a long shot.

Dr. Tierney said kids Sammy's age can feel like murderers if they were mad at the person who died. But Sam was never mad at Mom. When she was alive, you could ask Sam if he was having a good day, and he'd look at you like the question was retarded, and he'd say, "Every day is a good day." He really meant it—every single day of his life was a slice of Heaven. I don't think he would say that now. I don't know if he'll ever say that again.

I don't believe Sam put the snake in Mom's car. I asked Dad if he thought it might have been the crying guy. Dad said, "Why would Professor Johnston try to kill your mother?" I said, "I don't know. Maybe if he's a crazy stalker?" Dad gave me his confused smile. Then he asked, "Did your mother ever talk about him?" It was way obvious he suspected something was going on between them.

The crying guy is totally good-looking when he's not crying. Aunt Laura says that women like men who are tall, dark and handsome, and he's all three. Plus, she says that women like men who aren't afraid to show their feelings, which obviously he isn't, since he cried for hours in front of hundreds of people.

I said to Dad, "I never heard of the guy in my life, but he cried an awful lot at the funeral." And Dad said, "Hmm."

Friday, August 17th

We have to get to work on the scrapbook right away, because I'm already forgetting stuff. Today when Dad opened the door and shouted "Charlemagne!" I thought he'd gone insane. Like more than usual. I forgot that's our cat Charlie's full name. I don't know why Mom named him that. The real Charlemagne changed the face of Europe and conquered a whole empire. Our cat hasn't even conquered the yard—there's a bigger cat who pees on our porch regularly, and Charlie just runs inside when he comes around.

Our other cat is named after Cleopatra, the last pharaoh of ancient Egypt. She killed herself with an asp, which is a poisonous snake. That would have been the most horrible death Mom could have imagined.

If Mom were Cleopatra, she'd have drowned herself in the Nile.

Other people name a cat "Boots" because it has white feet, or "Ginger" because it's orange. Mom felt the need to name Cleo and Charlie after great historical leaders, even though all they do is sleep and eat and roll around all day biting each other's heads.

I miss talking to Mom about history. She would tell me about things she learned at work, or she'd ask what I was reading or which empire I was playing in *Civilization*. Then she'd tell me something cool about it or listen to me tell her something. Now there's no one to talk to.

There's no point in talking to Dad. Sam and I tried to interview him for the Mom Book, but he said that if he talked about Mom too much, he wouldn't be able to get up in the morning. That's a great thing to tell your four-year-old.

Dad's mental health must be seriously diving, because he asked if I want to go to church with him on Sunday. I've never been to church in my life, and I've never seen Dad go either. I told him the joke, "Why do you have to be quiet in church? Because people are sleeping." He said, all seriously, "That's disrespectful, Josh." Like he's a priest or something, when really he hasn't been in a church since the day he got married. Mom laughed her head off when I told her that joke.

Maybe Dad heard me teaching Sammy how to pray, so he thinks I'm dying to go to church. I'm working on a step-by-step plan to get Sam ready for kindergarten. Step One is, "Don't let Power Rangers talk out loud, especially not in a girly voice." Sam said Step One would be impossible to tackle at this point in his life. We moved on to Step Two, "Don't talk out loud to Mom, with or without the Ranger." Sam started to cry over the thought of Step Two.

I told him he could talk to Mom at the cemetery or in a church or praying by his bedside. I showed him how to pray. He thought it was the greatest thing. I told him he wasn't allowed to kneel down and pray wherever he happened to be, like in the mall or somewhere. I could totally see him doing that, and even if people think he's talking to God instead of his dead mother, it's still weird. He asked if he could talk to Mom just in his head, and I said okay. Maybe that'll be Step Six or something, but he's not ready for it yet. He's still in mourning.

Japanese Buddhists mourn for forty-nine days. If there's something unsolved about the person's death, like, say you don't know how a snake got in their car, the mourners say, "My forty-nine days are not over." That's exactly how I feel. My forty-nine days are not over. I feel like my forty-nine days will go on forever.

Sammy's beside me now, drawing in his journal. His profile looks like Mom's. She had long eyelashes and a round happy face. She was a happy person, like Sam. That's why it's so sad with her gone. She made up a large percentage of our family's happiness.

Sammy just let me see his journal, and I made him cry again. I skimmed the most recent pages. They're full of snakes scratched out. First he draws a snake, then he scratches it out. The one he's working on now is a snake attacking a person. I asked him if it was supposed to be Mom. He said, "No, it's Daddy." Then he asked if I would write in his journal that Daddy was killed in the car crash and snakes must be eliminated. Except Sammy called it "lemonated," which sounds like he wants to make them into a beverage.

I got mad and told him he was demented, and if Dad heard him it would break his heart. So of course Sammy bawled his eyes out. I got a grip and told him I was sorry. I said, "You're the best boy ever." He asked, "Better than you?" And I said, "Yeah, you're way better than me."

There's one drawing in Sam's journal that isn't scratched out. It shows the blue Power Ranger fighting a giant green snake. It looks like he put a lot of effort into it. I told him Mom would have loved that drawing, and he should be proud of it. He said Mom will be proud of him when he starts soccer and scores a hundred goals. I felt terrible because I'd forgotten all about that. I better talk to our neighbor about getting Sam on the team. Dr. Tierney said this is a bad time for disappointments and betrayals.

Speaking of disappointment, I got a letter back from Karen this morning. It was weird, like she was writing to a total stranger. It was only one page long. She said she'd heard from Simpson that I was back in soccer, but the rest of it was stuff about her camp. She said they heard an owl hoot in the night, and they tried to identify which species it was. She thought it was a great horned owl. Why would she write me about that? My mother just died. I couldn't care less which owl she heard. She didn't even ask how I'm doing. I think she doesn't like me anymore and she wishes she'd never kissed me. I'm not writing to her again. She comes home in a week anyway. I hope she still likes me, because it would be something to look forward to, but I wish she'd never written, because now I'm just depressed.

Sammy's bouncing on my bed right now, and the girl Power Ranger is laughing in a high-pitched hysterical scream. He's staring at her and laughing so hard I almost believe she's a real person instead of an eight-inch plastic doll. It's freakish, the sound he has her making. Like he has a split personality. He sure looks happy, in a demented sort of way.

There was a university student in Singapore who was bouncing on his bed listening to music and bounced himself right out the window. He fell three stories to his death and won a Darwin Award. I figure Mom's death was stupider than that guy's, so she'll probably get an award too. What's stupid about bouncing on a bed? I could use a good bounce right now. If I fell out the window, it wouldn't be stupid. It would just be an accident.

I was reading about evolution for my computer game, and I read a good monkey joke that Mom would have liked. It goes like this: A woman walks into a restaurant with her baby in a carriage. The waiter says to her, "That's the ugliest baby I've ever seen." The woman complains to the manager that the waiter insulted her. The manager apologizes. He tells her to choose something from the dessert counter for free to make up for being insulted. He says, "You go on up and see what we have. I'll stay here and watch your monkey."

That cracked me up. It would have cracked Mom up too. I told Dad, but he didn't even get it. He asked, "So was it really a monkey?" Duh. I don't know how Mom put up with his total lack of humor.

I tried the joke on Sammy just now, and he laughed his head off in two voices, which totally freaked me out. And he doesn't have a clue what the joke means.

Monday, August 20th

Sammy and I went around the neighborhood looking for scrapbook stories this weekend, and we introduced ourselves to the coach of five-year-old soccer. His daughter immediately fell in love with Sammy. They've never played together before—Sam never plays with girls because he's scared of them—but apparently Sam's insanity makes him more exciting than normal boys. They walked backward down the hallway about thirty-seven times, giggling. All three of them—Sammy and the girl and the Power Ranger.

Her name is Chloe. I told her that was almost the same as our cat's name, Cleo. She said, "My name's Chloe, not Cleo." Her dad laid his hand on my shoulder and said very politely, "It's not quite the same name." As if I were mentally retarded and needed to have that pointed out. He looked like he was about to explain the differences in vowel order, so I stepped away and asked if he had any cats. He seems like the kind of guy who'd own the big cat that scares Charlie and pees on our porch. But he said, "No, we don't have any pets." I find that suspicious.

He knew all about Mom dying. The first thing he said when he opened the door was, "Oh, boys, I'm so sorry about your mother." We've never spoken to the guy before in our lives. Maybe it's the kind of thing people talk about when they take out the garbage. "Did you hear? That nice lady across the street freaked out and drove into a tree."

I asked him if Sammy could join his soccer team. He laughed as if it were a joke, because registration was in April and there are only two games left in the season. The championship games are on Labor Day weekend, and we'll be away camping. We go to the same campsite every year—Mom books it in advance. I was honest about that. I told the coach that Sam would have to miss the tournament, which would only leave two games for him to play. He laughed and looked around like maybe he was on *Prank Patrol*. Then Sammy said, "Mommy likes soccer and she'll be proud of me when I score some goals." And the coach said, "Sure, you can join." Just like that.

He said he hopes the team welcomes Sammy. I don't think there'll be a problem. I've seen five-year-olds play soccer. Half of them look for worms in the dirt and the other half do handstands. They won't even notice Sammy joining the team. They'll probably think he played all season.

The coach said they play Tuesday evenings—which is tomorrow—but there are no more uniforms. Sammy was way disappointed at that, like it didn't count if he didn't have a uniform. So the coach said he'd find Sam a shirt with a number on it. Chloe said, "You better not give him my shirt." Her dad gave her a mean look and said, "It's the coach's decision." She said, "Then I won't have a shirt!" He said, "You have a mother." And that was the end of that conversation.

Sammy thought that was fair, that he should get the shirt since Chloe gets to have her mother. He was so happy he jumped up and down and hugged the coach, whose name is Carl Simpson, and who is not the sort of person you jump up and hug. I told him my best friend's first name was Simpson. He smiled politely and said, "Simpson is my *last* name." Like I might not know the difference between first names and last names because I'm mentally retarded. I just said "thanks" and left.

Sammy hugged Chloe good-bye, but then he practically had to break her fingers to get his Power

Ranger back. After that, they waved and smiled like they just loved each other. Little kids are so weird.

After that, we interviewed the neighbors about Mom. When I told Karen's mom we were making a scrapbook, she went into her house and brought out a box full of colored paper and stencils. Some of the papers are plain, but most have stripes or flowers or patterns on them. Karen's mom said we could use them for our scrapbook. She said she took classes on scrapbooking—it's an actual class you can take—and if we cut borders and titles out of different colored paper, our book would look more exciting.

I told her I never took classes in scrapbooking, but I took classes in computer programming. She said maybe she'll try that next time. Then she laughed like the idea was just ridiculous.

You'd think only kindergarteners would need a class in scrapbooking. But it was nice of her to give us the stuff. She said it was two hundred dollars' worth of paper. I find that hard to believe.

She didn't have many stories about Mom. She said Mom was pretty, and she made a face when she said it, like being pretty was just ridiculous. She only had two stories. Once, when I was in grade one, someone's mother was in an accident, so some of the other moms brought over food for the family. Karen's mom said my mom baked a couple of lasagnas.

I don't remember Mom ever baking lasagna in her life, so I said maybe she just bought them. Karen's mom said no, they were homemade. Whatever. I doubt it.

Her other story was about watching Mom do laps at the pool. She said she couldn't believe Mom was such a good swimmer. Mom looked like an Olympian, cutting through the water. Karen's mom stood by the wall for five minutes, just staring, because it was so beautiful to watch someone swim so well. I thought that was a way better story than the lasagna story. I'm going to include it in the scrapbook.

Mom used to swim all the way across the lake when we went camping. She'd move across the water with long slow strokes, like there was absolutely no chance she'd get tired or frightened in the middle of the lake with nothing to hold onto. She'd be in the sunshine on the very top of the water, getting smaller as she swam farther away, and I'd imagine the hundred feet of darkness underneath her, and all the creatures swimming in the dark. Mom would flip onto her back and wave at me from the middle of the lake. She knew I was a bit afraid of water.

But I never had a phobia. Our neighbor Mr. Smitts said he has a heights phobia so he knows what it's like to be too afraid to think straight. He said he wasn't afraid of heights until thirty years ago, when he took his daughter on a tiny Ferris wheel and freaked out.

He'd been up the CN tower before, and in airplanes and on big Ferris wheels, and he'd always liked it. But suddenly that day on the kiddie Ferris wheel, he was overwhelmed with fear. He screamed to get off. The guy running the machine thought it was funny, so he stopped them at the very top. Mr. Smitts tried to climb out of his seat until the guy brought them down again.

I said, "If you were afraid of heights, how could you be brave enough to climb down?" Mr. Smitts said, "I wasn't going to climb down. I was going to jump off. Just to get it over with." If he'd jumped, he'd have won a Darwin Award for sure, because how stupid is that? Mr. Smitts said no one can understand what a phobia is like until they feel it. He said you're not responsible when you're in that state of mind.

I told him about the university student who bounced out the window. He laughed and said that was a good way to die. I also told him about a guy who swallowed a fish on a dare and choked to death. Mr. Smitts said he almost chokes at every meal. I told him to have that checked out by a doctor, because that's just not normal.

Mr. Smitts had a lot of stories about Mom. He had so many stories, I think he's a stalker. He talked all day long about my mother. And all his stories were totally boring. He said when we first moved in, our dog would bark and make me cry. I told him the dog died before I was born, but he said no. Mom used to walk me and the dog at the same time, and I'd fall asleep in my stroller but the dog would bark and make me cry. That was one of his more exciting stories. He had other stories about Mom cleaning the windows. How dull is that?

He did have one really good story. Once, when I was little, Mom took me to Irene's Ice Cream shop along the bike path. There were three boys on bikes in the lineup in front of us who bought Freezies for fifty cents. Mr. Smitts said they'd spent the whole time in line talking about ice cream and drooling over all the flavors, so when they just bought little Freezies everyone felt sorry for them. They sat at a table outside and ate their Freezies, but they were still talking about the ice-cream flavors other people were buying. So Mom bought them all double-scoop cones, in chocolate and cotton-candy flavors. She asked the girl behind the counter to tell the boys they won them for being the hundredth customers that day. Those kids never even knew that it was my mom who bought them ice cream.

That story definitely belongs in the scrapbook. Nothing like that has ever happened to me. The other day Sammy and I were in the mall and I was drooling over the bikes, but nobody came up and said,

"Here, Josh, this bike's for you." I know ice cream is cheaper than bicycles but still, it was a very nice thing to do.

Interviewing Mr. Smitts took up most of Saturday and Sunday, and I'm not joking. This morning, Sammy and I took the bus to Mom's office, which is now the crying guy's office. He didn't cry this time, or even look like he might cry, so I should stop calling him that. He said I should call him Mitchell. I told him about our scrapbook, and how important it is because Sammy won't remember Mom when he's older. Mitchell said he would gather stories from the professors and students who knew Mom. He gave Sammy some highlighters for no good reason. Sam played with them while we were visiting, and Mitchell said he could take them home. Then he looked around and added a pen you can click to change the color of ink from black to red. I thought the pen was pretty cool, and maybe he should have given it to me, since Sammy only knows how to write one letter. But you can't compete with a four-year-old. I learned that a long time ago.

I might have been a little ticked off about the pen, because I blurted out the question, "Were you having an affair with our mom?" Mitchell looked surprised. I asked, "Did you put the snake in her car?" He looked even more surprised. He said, "No."

Then he said he loved my mom, and he would have asked her to marry him if she wasn't already married. I told him I didn't need to hear that. He said my mom loved my dad. I told him they did a lot of dancing in the kitchen. Then I asked, "So who put the snake in her car?" He grimaced like he was having stomach cramps, and he said we may never know.

Right about then, Sammy started talking to Mom through the Power Ranger, and I said we had to go see our psychiatrist. Mitchell asked, "Can I give you a lift?" I told him we were meeting Dad at his office two blocks away. Mitchell said, "Oh, that's right." Like he already knew where Dad worked, which is suspicious.

I talked to Dr. Tierney about how I'm tired of messing up the laundry—I now have ten socks that don't match, and my undershirts are pink. I talked about Sammy and how he can't be weird when school starts or his whole life will be ruined. Dr. Tierney said we shouldn't be parenting ourselves. I told him it'll be easier to find another mother than to get Dad to parent us properly. I don't want another mother, but Sam could use one.

Last night I found Dad in the basement watching home movies and crying. I didn't know we had any home movies, so I stayed and watched a few. There were some from before I was born and when

I was a baby, and when Sammy was born, and every year of our lives. They didn't make me cry at all. They made me really happy. We all looked happy in them. Not just one time, but over and over through all the years, we looked happy together. And that's a really good thing, even if one of us is dead now.

Before I saw the movies, I thought maybe we weren't happy together. Or at least maybe Mom wasn't happy, because she went and died. I thought someone as happy as she was in those movies wouldn't ram their car into a tree, even if they had a snake phobia. But now I think she just accidentally hit the tree. She didn't really want to leave us.

After the movies were over, I made fun of Dad's time machine, but he said, "I can do it, Josh." He was absolutely sure he could go back in time and change our whole lives. I left him there and came upstairs.

I looked around at our messy house. The recycling is overflowing. The garden is full of bugs, and the lawn is two feet tall—which Mr. Smitts mentioned, but not in a mean way. I opened some mail, and the bills haven't been paid, even though Dad still works. I know that for sure, because I'd thought maybe he was leaving the house every morning to hang out at the cemetery—which wouldn't have been a big surprise—so when we met him at work this morning, I asked the lady in the next office if Dad really worked every day. She said, "Yes, of course." So he should be able to pay the bills.

Dr. Tierney wouldn't talk to me about Dad, only about how I feel about Dad. I told him Dad's not as good as Mom, but he's better than nothing. I wish he'd just give up on his time machine. Last night when he was talking about it, I almost believed him for a second. I thought, *Maybe he'll do it! He'll go back and change things so Mom doesn't die!* But that's ridiculous.

But maybe it's not totally ridiculous. I don't know anything about time travel. I saw a funny movie where medieval knights come to modern America. I watched it with Mom a few years ago, and she loved it. It cracked us up. I should rent that movie again. I could use a good laugh.

It was nice having someone in the family who thought about me when I wasn't around. The day we watched that movie, I came home from Simpson's house and Mom said, "Hey, Josh, I rented a knight movie for us." She'd been thinking about me and doing something nice for me when I wasn't even there. That never happens anymore. Not that I go to Simpson's house anymore. He has two houses, and I don't go to either of them.

Simpson's mom drove us to soccer this weekend. Her ear was wrapped in a bandage. When I asked her about it, she gave Simpson a funny smile. She must have let him practice his piercing skills on her. I can't see Mom ever letting me do that, no matter how much she loved me. Simpson's mom is too nice for her own good. She would probably adopt us if I asked. But since she's already sad over Simpson's dad leaving, she doesn't need Sammy's insanity making her sadder. She cried when Simpson told her about Sam talking to Mom in the Power Ranger's girly voice.

I called Aunt Laura and asked her to visit again, because life is too hard without a mom around.

In most Native American tribes, families mourn for a whole year after a person dies. Aunts probably come around and help out a bit. The men in some tribes cut their hair as a sign of grief. I think that's a good practice. Sammy and I need haircuts before school starts.

Sammy has his first soccer game tomorrow at six o'clock. The coach dropped off his shirt tonight. It's number ten. Sammy wanted to sleep in it, but I said no. He's sitting up in bed right now, staring at it. He's so excited he probably won't sleep tonight. He'll probably bounce out the window, he's so excited. He'll probably choke to death.

Friday, August 24th

The decisions that turn out to be important in your life aren't always about important things. "Do I go skydiving?" is something you'd take your time deciding. But other decisions seem too small to matter. Like, "Should I have a look under the driver's seat to make sure there's no snakes in the car that'll scare me stupid when I'm on the highway going a hundred kilometers an hour between a concrete barrier and a hardwood forest?" Who would ponder that?

There's no word yet on whether Mom will get a Darwin Award. I didn't put a proper subject on my e-mail. I chose the "Miscellaneous" category. I asked if someone would qualify if they died because of a phobia. I gave Mom's example, and I provided a list of smart things she did, like writing two books on medieval plays that stupid people never even heard of.

Mitchell came by our house on Wednesday night with a file box full of stories about Mom from the people she worked with—students and professors and secretaries and even the cleaners, who said Mom was friendly and kept her office neat. One story was totally weird. It was about a student named Ben who had a crush on Mom. He sent her flowers and presents every day. He dropped by her office and hung around outside her classes and creeped people out. Mom wasn't even nice to him—she took out a restraining order and acted like he was invisible. I thought he must be the one who put the snake in her car. But Mitchell told me Ben was in jail at the time for attacking another student. That says a lot.

I told Mitchell I'd read that one in eight female university students are stalked every year. I asked him if he thought that was true. He said, "Yes. You wouldn't believe how many young men are basically insane, Josh." I thought that was a very negative thing for a professor to say. Then Sammy ran up, and the girl Power Ranger kissed Mitchell's arm and said, "Stay with us, my dear and true friend." Mitchell just nodded like that was his closing argument.

Sammy's Power Ranger never stutters. I mentioned this to Dad, and he asked, "Why would she stutter?"

I said, "Because Sammy stutters." Dad said, "Sammy doesn't stutter." I said, "I-I-I-I think he-ee-ee-ee-he does." Dad said, "Oh, that. That's not a stutter."

Since two out of three men in my family are insane, Mitchell is probably right to believe the crazy-stalker statistics.

It was very nice of him to bring the stories over. He typed them up and printed them out with headlines and clip art and put it all in a report cover. We're calling it the Professor Book. It's mostly boring, and the stories have nothing to do with me and Sammy or Dad. They don't belong in the Mom Book. Even if Mom were alive, we'd never know those stories, unless we found out about the stalker guy when he got out of jail.

Mitchell put his own story in the collection, and it wasn't about how much he adored Mom. It was about how Mom adored me and Sammy so much that she made the other teachers want to have kids. Mitchell knows all the details of our lives. He knows that Sammy likes the red Power Ranger best—although anybody could guess that, because the red Ranger is always the best. He also knows about tiny things, like Sammy's Scooby-Doo flashlight and how he sneaks into Mom's bed and annoys the cats with it every night. Except now he sneaks into my bed.

Mitchell knows that Cleo's full name is Cleopatra and Charlie's full name is Charlemagne, which even

I'd forgotten. He teaches a course on the real Charlemagne. He also plays *Civilization*—which is weird because he's forty, and he's tall, dark and handsome, so you'd think he'd be going out with women instead of playing games all day. Whatever. He knows that I'm an expert player and that I want to make games when I'm older.

He said he liked making the Professor Book. "It's a wonderful way to honor someone you love," he said, right in front of Dad. Dad winced at the word "love."

I asked Mitchell what Roman Catholic people do to mourn the dead. He said he didn't know because he's not a practicing Catholic, whatever that means. His father died when he was young, and his mother planted a tree as a memorial. They decorate it with lights on his dad's birthday every year. But that's not a Roman Catholic practice. It's just what his family does.

There was a strange moment when Mitchell first arrived. I shouted down the basement for Dad, and Sammy said, "Daddy's building his time machine." At first Mitchell thought it was a joke, but then he realized our dad was actually in the basement ignoring us and building a time machine. He said, "Why?" Sammy smiled and stuttered, "So he-e-e can take the-the-the snake out of the car." It was hard for me not to cry. A lot of times Sammy says something sad without knowing it, because he's too little.

Before Mitchell left, he told me there's an exhibit on Albert Einstein at the Museum of Nature that I should go see with my dad. As if Dad's still a regular person who goes anywhere besides work and the basement. I might check it out by myself. I don't know much about Einstein.

I asked Mitchell if he knew any available mothers for Sam, since we obviously need one. He could probably tell that by our shrunken gray clothes and our house that smells like cat litter and the fact that we were eating popcorn for supper when he arrived. He said he'd keep his eye out. He doesn't need a wife as badly as Dad does.

Mitchell is divorced but he's not a father, so he's not too depressed. All the divorced fathers I know drink beer at lunchtime and try to make dates with total strangers in grocery store lineups. Ameer's dad is a mess, and Karen's dad is almost as bad. They can't even dress themselves properly. They make bad jokes to pretty women and never take the hint.

Simpson's dad is normal because he ran to a new wife—which is not nice for Simpson's mom, but at least he's not annoying strangers all over town. He'll be driving us to soccer tonight, which is never as much fun as when Simpson's mom drives. I'd bet a million bucks he won't have any piercing wounds anywhere on his body.

Since Dad is a widower, he doesn't bother women the way divorced fathers do. But as a parent, he's much worse than average. Even though he shouldn't get married for a year, according to the Jewish rules, it wouldn't hurt to check out what mothers are available. In our scrapbook interviews, I've added a question about whether anyone knows a nice woman to be Sammy's new mom. By focusing on Sammy, and ignoring me and Dad, we'll have a better shot at success. Sammy is totally cute and in obvious need of maternal care. Who wouldn't want to be his mom?

He was awesome at his soccer game on Tuesday! I couldn't believe it! He was totally normal and not weird at all. He talked to the other kids and listened to the coach and went on and off the field when he was told. He didn't even pick up the soccer ball with his hands, like he does when we play in the yard. He kept the Power Ranger in his pocket. I could see his hand in there and his lips moving through the game, but you'd never guess what he was doing if you didn't already know about his insanity. He was absolutely great. He didn't shout, "This one's for you, Mom!" before he took a shot at goal, which I was half expecting him to do.

Aunt Laura came to his game. She's coming over tomorrow for the whole day. "To get things under control," she said. When she picked us up for

Sammy's soccer, she made a face at the stench of cat pee. She spent a long time talking to Dad. They were too quiet to hear, but a couple of times she raised her voice. Once she yelled, "You can't travel back in time!" And once she yelled, "Your children look like orphans!" That was a bit harsh because, even though I've blended the colors in the wash, at least we're not in our pajamas anymore.

Sam just peeked into my room and asked to come to my game tonight, but I had to say no. He asked, "Why not?" I said, "Because Simpson's dad doesn't like children." He asked, "Why doesn't Daddy take us?" I said, "Sam, I really have no idea."

Saturday, August 25th

Somehow Aunt Laura made Dad change the cat litter and clean the bathroom and come to my soccer game tonight. He didn't sit in the stands reading a book either. He tried to, but she grabbed his book and shook her head. Not like she felt sorry for him, which is how most women shake their heads at Dad. Aunt Laura knows that Dad used to read books at my games way before Mom died. It's not like he's stopped paying attention to us or taking us out. Just like he hasn't stopped cleaning the bathroom or changing the cat litter. He never did those things in the first place. He can't get it through his head that he has to do them now. Aunt Laura says he should have done them even when Mom was alive.

It was nice to have everyone at my game for a change. Sammy cheered in stereo each time I scored. Instead of sounding like an insane child with the split personality of his dead mother, it sounded very cool and musical. He cheered, "Way to go, Josh!" in his own voice, then, "That's my boy!" in the girly voice, with two claps in between. It caught on. Half the team was cheering in two voices by my third goal.

After the game, the coach let me and Sammy kick a ball around the field. Sam scored two goals on me. I was going easy on him, but he did well. He's faster than I remembered. He's been walking backward for so long, I forgot how fast he can run forward.

We bought drive-through ice-cream cones after the game and took them to the park. Our neighbor was there—Sam's coach, Mr. Simpson, as in "Simpson is my *last* name"—with his daughter, Chloe. She was up on the rubber tires of the jungle gym, and her dad was saying, "Aren't you going to come down the slide? Why don't you come down the slide?" Parents always do that. Once a kid finds something they actually want to do, the parents try to get them to do something else. "Oh my god, you're having too much fun up there, you better come down."

When Sammy finished his cone, he climbed up the jungle gym to play with Chloe. Five seconds later they were rolling down the slide on top of each other.

They kissed and ran around backward holding hands. It was so cute, I couldn't stop laughing. Seriously, I was worried I might never stop. I got that weird hysteria thing where in the middle of a laugh you think you might cry like a baby.

The same thing happened to Dad, and he actually did start to cry. Big heaving sobs that made Mr. Simpson walk halfway across the park to get away from him. Dad was all hunched over shuddering. I shouted out that it was just an allergy attack and not to worry.

When he calmed down to a regular cry, Dad said he was sad because Mom wasn't there to see us—to see me scoring at my game and Sammy kissing a girl in the park. He said every happy moment with us in the whole future of our lives will hold the sadness for him that Mom isn't there to see it. I have to admit, that's a good reason to cry.

Earlier today, Sammy and I went around taking pictures and making drawings for the Mom Book, so we'll have a record of places like Mom's garden and the bike path and the park bench she liked best. While we were out, I saw Karen walking up the street with a towel under her arm. She must be back from camp. I shouted her name, and she looked around and saw me, but she didn't wave. I shouted again, but that time she didn't even look. I asked Sammy if he wanted to go to the pool, but he said no because swimming causes drowning.

I hope he's not getting a phobia about swimming. Phobias can start out as rational fears—like a fear of drowning when you're not a good swimmer. The more you let the fear scare you, the more it becomes crazy and irrational. I read that phobias are the most common mental-health problem in North America. That's really hard to believe, because Mom and Mr. Smitts are the only two people I've ever met with a phobia, whereas psychos are everywhere.

The most common phobias are of animals— especially dogs, mice, insects and snakes—plus storms, heights and closed-in spaces. I had never heard of a fear of storms before. It's called *brontophobia*. There are many rare phobias too. Like *dentophobia*, which is a fear of going to the dentist. Nobody likes going to the dentist, but some people spend years in agony with their teeth rotting out because they're so afraid to go.

There's *papyrophobia*, which is a fear of paper. People with that phobia will run away from news-paper stands, or they'll leave a restaurant where someone is reading the paper. Maybe the woman who jumped off the bus to have a cigarette was actu-ally papyrophobic and somebody beside her cracked open the comics.

Maybe papyrophobics were hit on the head with a rolled-up newspaper when they were little. Or maybe they watched their parents hit the dog they loved with a newspaper. How else could you become afraid of paper?

Some people are so phobic they can't even leave the house, and they spend their whole lives alone and afraid. They start off as normal people. Maybe they're afraid to speak in public, but they have to do a speech for school. They totally bomb, and their fear gets worse. Then they go to the mall, and a pretty girl asks for directions. They stutter and the girl laughs at them, and their fear gets even worse. Eventually going anywhere feels so awful they can't do anything except stay home.

I have to make sure Sammy doesn't become one of those sad people. He should eliminate his fears by facing them one at a time. He seems to be totally over his fear of little girls—but since that took thirty seconds with Chloe to overcome, I'm guessing it wasn't a real phobia. It can take years of therapy to get over a real one.

I told Aunt Laura about behavior-modification therapy for overcoming phobias. I said Mom should have done that. Aunt Laura patted my hand and said, "Josh, honey, half the people on the road would lose control of their cars if a snake slithered out between their feet." She's probably right. It would freak you out even if you liked snakes. Dad nearly crashed the car and killed us all once when a bee flew in through the window and landed on his thigh. He totally spazzed out, and he's not even apiophobic, which means afraid of bees.

Whoever put the snake in Mom's car might not even have known about her phobia. That makes the list of suspects practically endless.

I just shut my light off and looked at the stars, but then I realized we missed the Perseids meteor shower two weeks ago, so now I'm bummed. This year there was no moon on August twelfth, which is the peak of the shower, so we would have seen a million shooting stars. It happens every August and it's named after the constellation Perseus, the Greek hero. At Mom's university, in the office across from hers, there's a poster of Perseus holding up Medusa's head. Mom couldn't even look in that direction because of the snakes. It was a creepy poster, partly because of the severed head, but mostly because Perseus was totally naked, which is a weird way to fight monsters.

Every August when the Perseids happened, Mom and I would drive out to an abandoned farm outside of town where the light pollution isn't bad, and we'd lie down on a pile of blankets to watch the meteor shower. Once all four of us went, but Sammy was so afraid of the dark he ruined it by saying, "I hear something coming," every two seconds. So usually just Mom and I went. This year would have been especially great with no moon.

It still happened—the meteors fell all over the sky—but I didn't see it. There's tons of stuff like that happening right now. There's a new IMAX movie, and new exhibits at the museums, and maybe even a fair. Life is going on around me, but I'm missing it all. Like that Einstein exhibit Mitchell told me about. Mom would have already taken me to that.

I'll have to start reading the newspaper. Mom was the only person in my family who ever knew what was going on.

Monday, August 27th

I called Karen yesterday, but her mom said she wasn't home. I think she was lying. I called Simpson and he said, "Yeah, Karen's back from camp but I haven't seen her." I can't tell if he's lying.

I read a book about phobias. I feel sorry for people who have them. Like *selenophobia*, a fear of the moon, or *chionophobia*, a fear of snow. I'm always happy to see the moon, and I get excited every time it snows. People with phobias never have those great feelings.

There's a fear of walking, called *basiphobia*, and even a fear of thinking, called *phronemophobia*. You'd be a total mental case if you were scared to death of thinking.

The fear of snakes is called *ophidiophobia*, and it's pretty common.

Napoleon Bonaparte, the famous French general, was ailurophobic, which means afraid of cats. If all those people he conquered had let out their house-cats, maybe he'd have run away. I can picture Charlie and Cleo chasing Napoleon back to his ship, with his crazy hat falling off his head as he ran, and the two cats all fierce and proud of living up to their names at last.

People with phobias need to exercise to release stress. The book recommended walking, but if you had *basiphobia* or you were in a hurry, you could try biking instead. If Mom had biked to her office that day, she'd have released her stress and not crashed the car. But who knows? Maybe a snake sunning itself on the bike path would have made her spaz out and crash into a three-year-old tricyclist and kill him. Then she'd have killed herself out of guilt. So there'd be two families destroyed instead of just one. You can never say for sure that the horrible thing that's happening to you is the worst thing possible. It could always be worse. But it could be better too. She could have just pulled the car over.

I was working on the scrapbook this weekend, sorting through photos and putting stories in order. I remembered a story Mom told me just before Sam turned four. She took him to the store to pick up his birthday cake—which was a Scooby-Doo cake,

no surprise there—and he started crying on the
way home. He was in the car seat beside his cake
box, happy as can be, when all of a sudden he
started bawling his eyes out. Mom thought maybe
he'd crushed the cake. But no, it was fine. She asked
him, "What's wrong?" And he said, "I don't want to
get older." He said he wanted to stay three years old
forever, but with cake and presents. I can totally relate
to that. Life is good when you're three years old.

Mom said she wished we could stay little forever.
She called it a selfish wish. She said she should want
us to grow into adults who find our place in the world
and have families of our own. But in her heart, she
wanted to keep us small and together. "In the center
of each other's lives," she called it. I told her that
wasn't a selfish wish at all, because Sammy was probably happier at three than he'd ever be again in his life.
I said I was probably happier when I was three too.
I asked if she was happier as a grown-up, with her
work and us and Dad, or as a little girl with Grandma.
She said she didn't remember being a little girl.

It sucks that you can't remember. I honestly
believe the first five years of life are the best. You're
happy doing anything. Cutting construction paper is a
really good time when you're three. You play with toys
all day and you're really into it, not just pretending.
Everyone makes a big deal of everything you do.

They tell you you're great because you poop in a toilet. How can you top that kind of admiration? Plus you're with your mom all the time, and she adores you and looks at you like she couldn't possibly be happier than she is with you. Unless you have a rotten mother, in which case it would totally suck to be three and you couldn't wait to grow up. But if you have a nice mom, it's great. Until your nice mom dies. Then it sucks.

It's eight o'clock in the morning, and I should feed the cats. I didn't sleep much last night because we have an incredibly important day today. We're going to meet Sammy's kindergarten teacher. Dad took the morning off work. He's in the shower right now. Sam's supposed to bring his school supplies to the classroom—except we haven't bought them yet—and we get a tour of the building and meet the teacher, whose name Dad can't remember. He can't find the letter about it, but he knows the meeting is at ten o'clock, because he wrote it in his agenda. That gives us time to buy school supplies.

Mom used to lay out all our supplies on the kitchen table the night before school started. She'd label every single pencil and pack them up one by one and tick them off the supply list, as if it was an emergency kit like the kind people keep in bomb shelters, and if I only got one glue stick instead of two, everything would fall to pieces.

The rest of us are totally disorganized compared to her. I can't believe that Dad makes maps at work. You'd think a person would have to be organized for that. I'm surprised Dad doesn't get the capital cities mixed up, or put the mountains in the wrong places, or leave whole countries off the map.

I'm going with him to meet Sammy's teacher, even though the letter didn't invite siblings. I figure it will take at least me and Dad to make up for one organized parent. Even with both of us, there's a good chance we'll come out of the meeting and not remember the teacher's name. We told Sam that was his job.

Sammy just walked into my room wearing new clothes. Really nice, clean things with no wrinkles or stains. I have no idea where they came from. He said Mom put them on his bed. He didn't actually say "Mom." He said, "My mommy." Like we've each got our own. He always says that. Dad used to ask, "So how was your day, Sam?" And Sammy would say, "My mommy met me for lunch." And Dad would look at Mom just to make sure she was the mommy Sam was talking about.

It's not possible that Mom put new clothes on Sam's bed, so where did they come from?

It was Dad who put the clothes on Sam's bed. He went shopping yesterday. He bought clothes for me too, but he can't remember where he put the bags. I asked, "Why didn't you buy the school supplies at the same time?" He looked at me like maybe I was expecting a bit much and getting the clothes was out of character enough.

We bought Sam a Power Rangers schoolbag and a Scooby-Doo pencil case and a Transformers lunch box—even though he's never even seen Transformers. And pencils with happy faces on them, and purple glue sticks, and his whole list of supplies. He was thrilled with his new things, and the cashiers were smiling over how adorable he is.

His teacher is named Madame Denis. When Sammy heard that, he told her the joke, "Knock-knock." "Who's there?" "Madame." "Madame who?" "Madame toot's caught in the door." Then he exploded with laughter. Madame Denis just shook her head and said, "We don't say that word in school." Sammy asked, "What word?" Madame Denis glared at Dad like he was an incompetent parent.

She helped Sam take his supplies out of his bag to keep at school. She told him to take the lunch box and schoolbag home and bring them back and forth every day. "Like Josh does," Sammy said. Madame Denis gave me a look that said I better not forget

my lunch box or I'll be hearing from her. She gave
Dad a list of lunch suggestions, because there's a kid
in Sam's class who's allergic to peanuts, so you have
to bring alternatives. There's stuff on the list like
chicken drumstick and *pasta salad* and food I never
once got in my lunch even when Mom was alive.
There's a cafeteria at the junior high school, so I can
buy lunch. In kindergarten they have pizza Fridays,
but all the other days they have to bring a packed
lunch. I can't see Dad fixing up a chicken drumstick
and pasta salad, so we'll stock up on microwavable
Chef Boyardee.

Madame Denis is very strict. She won't let Sammy
walk backward in school. Not in the classroom, not
in the hall, not outside, not anywhere. She said it's
dangerous. She said, without the least bit of sympathy,
"It would make your mother cry to see you walking
backward." Just like that. And she never even met
our mother.

She said, "There are better ways to keep people
alive in your heart." I told her about the scrapbook
we're making. She said it sounds lovely and when it's
done Sam can bring it into class one time if he wants.

She said, "You can also remember someone by
wearing something special, either something they
owned or made, or a locket with their picture in it."
She opened up her necklace and showed us a picture

of a little girl. She didn't say if it was her daughter or her sister or whoever, but I'm guessing it's someone dead.

I told her that was a good idea, but Sammy doesn't walk backward to remember Mom. He walks backward to remember all the people who are still alive, so if they die he'll remember their faces. She said, "Nonsense." Just like that. She said if you walk backward you have to think too much about where you're going to properly concentrate on what you're seeing. She said instead of walking backward, when Sammy leaves a room or says good-bye to someone, he can take a pretend picture with his fingers, then turn around and walk forward to wherever he's going.

I think the pretend picture thing is just as weird as walking backward, but maybe it's more acceptable among kindergarteners.

Madame Denis said we have no idea who's going to die. Maybe it's not the person you're leaving who'll die, but the person you're heading toward. So you should walk in the safest way possible, and forward is the only way allowed in school.

She said she certainly hoped that Dad didn't let Sammy walk backward on the roads or sidewalks. Dad shrugged and said he bought new school clothes. She seemed to take that as a good answer.

Madame Denis has some special kind of kinder-garten-teacher power, because Sammy is now walking forward. He turns around to take imaginary pictures, but that's still a big improvement. And it only took twenty minutes with Madame Denis for Sam to master. She'll have him totally normal by Christmas.

On the way home from kindergarten, we stopped at the garden center and bought a tree for Mom, like Mitchell's family has for his father. I wanted a rose-bush, but Dad said we'd kill it with too much water or not enough light, and then we'd feel terrible. So we bought a cedar tree instead. Mom liked the way cedars twist into different shapes and the way they smell. We're going to plant it in the middle of the front yard, where it will have lots of room to grow. We're calling it Mom's Tree.

In Europe, you can have yourself composted when you die, then mulched into soil and put under a tree, so your memory tree is actually feeding on what's left of your body. I find that very sick and gross, but I read that it's becoming popular. The planet is running out of space to bury people. In some cities, instead of buying a grave forever, you rent one for fifty years. They dig you up after you've decomposed and everyone has stopped visiting you, and they put a new dead person there. That wouldn't work for Mom, because Sammy and I will still be alive in fifty years.

I don't want to show up at the grave and find a stranger buried there.

Except we never visit Mom's grave. Sammy's scared of graveyards, and it's too far for me to bike. Plus it's where I made a total idiot of myself. I still can't stand the thought of her body under all that earth. I might freak out again and try to dig her up, and I don't think Dr. Tierney is prepared to handle that.

If we have Mom's Tree and her scrapbooks, maybe we should have just rented the grave. I don't intend to ever go near the place. The idea of the person you love all rotten and wormy under the ground is totally gross. But not as gross as feeding them to your tree.

At the garden center, while Dad was talking to some woman, acting like a pathetic divorced man, Sammy dropped his Power Ranger in a tub of pinwheels and freaked out. I thought he'd been stabbed in the heart while I wasn't looking, or maybe one of his eardrums exploded or his eyeball fell out. I spent five minutes checking him for wounds before I figured out why he was screaming. Dad rushed over, and we had to dump all the pinwheels out of the tub to reach the Power Ranger. The clerk was angry, but the pinwheels were plastic so it's not like they got ruined from being on the floor. We put them all back.

We have to cure Sam of his Ranger obsession. Dad said he could take the toy to a jeweler to make into a necklace so Sam wouldn't lose it again. But that won't work. It's too big to tuck under a shirt. Everyone would say, "Hey, kid, there's a Power Ranger hanging from your neck." And Sam would say, "Yeah, that's my dead mom." And presto, he'd be the weird kid.

I said we could buy some Power Ranger underwear to replace the doll, but Sammy looked at me like that was just sick and wrong. I don't know what we'll do. I doubt if he'll ever lose the toy by forgetting where he put it, because he honestly never lets go of it. But he might set it down for a second to pull his boots on, and it could get kicked across the floor accidentally. Then some kid would take it home. Kids steal things all the time. Someone stole my Yu-Gi-Oh! cards when I snuck them to school in grade four to duel at lunchtime.

While Dad was bothering the woman in the garden center, Sammy told me he doesn't ever want a new mom. I called Mitchell at his office this afternoon to tell him to stop looking. That was weird, because it's Mom's old phone number. Mitchell asked how my dad was doing, and I said, "He's busy with work and the time machine." I told him about Sam's new clothes and how Dad came to my soccer game and cleaned the litter box. Mitchell said he's sure that Dad will come around eventually.

I told him that Native Americans take a year to mourn, and Mitchell said, "Yeah, you already told me that." I told him the joke about what did the Buddha say to the hot-dog vendor, and he said, "Yeah, your mom told me that." So I said, "What did the hot dog say when it won the race?" He said, "I don't know. What?" I said, "I'm the wiener!" And he laughed.

Wednesday, August 29th

This day keeps getting worse and worse.

First thing in the morning I saw Karen at the park. She said, "Hi, Josh," and then she walked away. I thought, *I'm not taking this.* I ran after her and asked why she was ignoring me. "You don't have to be my girlfriend," I said. "Or even my friend. But since we've known each other since grade two, you can't just ignore me." She took a big breath. I thought for sure she was going to tell me she likes Simpson—because he always changes the subject when I talk about her lately—but she didn't. She told me about people she met at camp, kids I don't even know. Then Sammy introduced her to his Power Ranger. "A snake killed my mom," he said. Karen ran home without even speaking to him. She's usually really nice to Sammy, so go figure that one.

I don't understand why she doesn't like me anymore. Maybe I was mean to her when Mom first died. I yelled at almost everyone back then. Maybe it creeps her out to remember me freaking at the funeral. Or maybe it's just that I'm grungy and I need a haircut. She must like another guy, maybe Simpson or someone she met at camp. She was away for six weeks, and that's plenty of time to meet someone else. I wish she'd have the guts to tell me about him. Stringing me along like this is mean.

When she told me she liked me at graduation, she didn't just say she liked me. She said she's always liked me, ever since we were little kids. When you like someone for years and you finally kiss them, you shouldn't ditch them for some guy at camp. I've liked Karen for years, and I could meet a hundred girls at camp and I'd still like her. Maybe she was lying when she said she always liked me. Maybe she was just being nice and now she regrets it. I really don't know.

One thing I know is that you can't travel back in time. That was the next rotten thing in my day. I went to the Museum of Nature and saw the Albert Einstein exhibit. I've never been to a museum without Mom before. The security guard stalked me the whole time I was there. I could understand it if Sammy were with me, trying to touch the artifacts. But I biked over on my own. It was the weirdest coincidence, because Cheetah was there with Jim. I saw them in the dinosaur section. Cheetah ran over and gave me a hug and kissed my cheek. The security guard stopped stalking me after that. I guess he thought they were my parents, even though Cheetah would have been about thirteen when I was born.

They went through the Einstein exhibit with me. I learned two things. First, Albert Einstein was Jewish, so he would have mourned his dead mom for a year. Second, his theory of general relativity doesn't allow for backward time travel—except maybe in unusual situations like the presence of negative energy, which is antimatter, and which there's definitely none of in my basement.

A display called *Can We Ever Go Back?* listed the time-travel theories of different physicists. They pretty much all said no. The bottom of the display panel read: *It is currently unknown if the laws of physics would allow for travel back in time.* Dad's time machine is doomed.

It's theoretically possible to go forward in time, but backward is unscientific. Backward is a leap of faith, and I have no faith—not Jewish or Muslim or Christian or Hindu, not time-travel faith like Dad, and not Power Ranger faith like Sammy. I wish I had some kind of faith, but I don't. Not even forward-time-travel faith like Albert Einstein. It's impossible to go back or forth in real life. Albert Einstein was Jewish and he was from Germany, so his relatives were probably all killed by the Nazis. I bet he wished he could zoom them forward to a time when the Nazis were defeated. But he couldn't. We're all stuck right here and now, and there's no getting around it.

Except if you wake up one day and your wife dies, and then you bury her and go down into your basement to build a time machine, and you stay down there, ignoring your kids for years. One day, when you came up from the basement, your kids would be grown and gone, and it would be like you traveled forward in time. And it would be wrong.

Part of me deep down was hoping we could go back in time. When I read that it's impossible, there was a thud in my chest, like something dropping down a well. Jim put my bike in Cheetah's trunk and they drove me home. They tried to cheer me up, but I was so sad I didn't say anything except good-bye.

When I got home, Aunt Laura was mad because she thinks I'm too young to go into the city alone. She was sick of babysitting Sammy. She spoke in very short sentences with her voice snapping like a wet towel. It's true that Sam can be tiring these days. I said, "Thanks for babysitting. You can go home now. I'll get supper." She said, "No. I'm waiting for your father." She was obviously waiting to start a fight with him.

I tried to think of something happy to take my mind off Karen and Einstein. I told Aunt Laura how Madame Denis suggested Sam and I should choose something of Mom's to remember her by. Aunt Laura said, "Oh, all right." She sighed like it was a huge effort for her to walk up the stairs, even though we didn't want her to come up with us.

It started off okay. I found a plain gold chain with a glass pendant in the shape of a tree. Mom bought it in the market from a local artist. It's not girly—it's a tree, so it could be for anyone. Since we have Mom's Tree to plant, it's a perfect memory to wear. So that was my choice.

The problem began when Sam chose Mom's bathrobe as his memory. Aunt Laura started huffing like the Big Bad Wolf. She said no, the bathrobe was too big, and Sammy should pick something else. Those weren't her exact words. Her exact words were, "Don't be an idiot. It's huge." I got mad, because it wasn't her idea to wear something of Mom's, so she shouldn't be the judge. Plus we've always had a rule of "no name-calling" in our house. You have to say, "I think that's an idiotic idea," instead of, "You're an idiot." The bathrobe wasn't a good choice—it's even bigger than the Power Ranger—but that's no reason to be mean.

Sammy explained that on Sunday mornings when he got up to watch TV, he would sit on Mom's lap, and if it was cold she'd wrap her robe around both of them and tie the belt over Sam's belly. That's a nice memory to put in the scrapbook, but he had to make another choice. A kid who wears his dead mother's robe is labeled for life. Plus he'd trip over it and fall down and smash his face in.

I told Sam to choose from the jewelry box instead. Aunt Laura picked up a pearl ring and said, "Wow, this is pretty. Can I have it?" I should have been nicer, but it's not her stuff and she can't just take it, so I said no. She totally spazzed out. She started yelling that it's been two months since Mom died and we should get rid of her stuff. She took Mom's clothes out of the closet and threw them on the bed. Sammy and the Power Ranger started screaming. I stood in front of Mom's clothes like I was protecting them, and I told Aunt Laura to leave us alone. She yelled, "You're already alone so much you've gone crazy!" That may be true, but it's not like she was helping the situation.

That's when Dad walked in. He had just gotten home from work. He grabbed Aunt Laura by the arms and shouted, "Don't touch her things!" Then he said more quietly, "Thank you for watching Sam, but now you should leave." She said, "You can't keep her things forever!" I said, "Our forty-nine days are not over." She looked at the three of us like we're insane, and then she left.

We went outside to plant Mom's Tree. It took Dad an hour to dig a big enough hole. Sammy kept saying, "That's good, Daddy," and dragging the tree over and breaking off the green bits. Dad yelled at us to go to the park while he dug the hole. He yells way more than he used to. I'm starting to suspect he's not a cyborg after all.

Things got even worse at the park.

Sammy was rocking on the metal pig. Darren, the four-year-old bully, was playing in the sand with some cars. Darren's mom was sitting on the bench talking on her cell phone. I started running up the slide to work off my stress. Suddenly I heard a high-pitched shriek, and I saw Darren run across the grass with Sammy tearing after him. I could not believe how fast Sam ran. It was like he was propelled by a rocket. It reminded me of a nature show where the cheetah springs up out of nowhere and races through the savannah and tackles the baby antelope.

Man, did Sammy tackle Darren when he caught up to him! He plowed him into the grass and pummeled him. He slammed his fists into the kid's face and screamed in his crazy high-pitched shriek. I ran up to them and pulled Sammy off. It was like holding back a wild dog. By the way he'd been punched, I thought for sure Darren's face would be bloody and unrecognizable, with broken teeth and black eyes and his lip hanging off and everything. But no. The kid looked totally normal except for a grass stain on his cheek.

Sam started kicking Darren and yelling, "Give it back!" I saw that Darren had Sam's Power Ranger. He got up and ran away with it.

This time I chased him down. I pinned his arm to his side and pried the Ranger loose while he slapped at me with his free hand. I wanted to punch him, but he's only four and that would be wrong. I just took the toy back. When I held it out to Sammy, Darren tried to snatch it again. So I held it up high. The kid jumped for it like a dog, which freaked me out a bit. Sammy slammed him to the ground and started hitting him again. He pushed him down so hard you'd think it would have broken the kid's back. But no. Darren was fine. He was almost smiling.

I had to drag Sammy home by the wrist, because he kept trying to run back and beat the crap out of Darren some more. Darren stood in the park watching us go. All this time his mom was talking on her phone, just gabbing away. It was the weirdest thing.

When we got home, Dad was finished digging the hole, but he had to drive back to the garden center for soil. Sammy and I held the tree straight while Dad poured in the dirt and tamped it down until finally the tree stood up instead of tipping over.

It was sunset by the time we went inside, so we ordered pizza. While we waited for it to be delivered, we went through Mom's jewelry for memories.

Dad said his wedding ring is his memory. I realized that Mom's watch could be my memory, since I wear it all the time. But I chose the tree pendant anyway. The watch is more of a practical thing. Sammy picked a macaroni necklace he made for Mom in preschool. Half the macaronis are chipped, and red paint comes off in your hand if you hold it too long. Whatever. It's his choice. Then Dad called Aunt Laura and left a message saying he was sorry for yelling at her.

Dad seems different now, and I mean better. It's like he's on our side—mine and Sammy's—instead of alone. Even though it was a rotten day from morning till night, I don't feel so bad. Maybe we're not totally hopeless.

Saturday, September 1st

It's Labor Day weekend and we're camping. When we used to camp with Mom, we'd hike and do scavenger hunts and collect shells and tell ghost stories. Now, without Mom, we're sitting at the campsite, writing in our psychiatrist journals. We're not even sitting around a campfire, because we have no campfire. Mom was the one good at fires. The wood they sell here is all giant logs with no kindling and we have no ax. Mom would have found a way to make a fire with just a match and a tree, but none of us can. We have seven logs lying in the firepit. I guess we'll just go in the tent when it gets dark, like we did last night.

We arrived at three minutes to sundown yesterday because Dad forgot that Mom isn't around to pack for us. He thought we could just grab some ice bags and be on our way. But there's no point in ice without food and a cooler. We shopped for burgers and corn on the cob. Then we packed our clothes and found the tent—which was in the very back of the shed and smells like the cats have peed on it. By the time we got here it was almost dark.

It's a good thing Mom booked the site last year, because there was a long lineup of campers waiting for cancellations. There were cars packed to the roof with sleeping bags and beach umbrellas, with grumpy tired people leaning against them scowling. They'd gone to all the trouble of packing when they didn't even have a campsite. They gave us dirty looks as we drove in. If we'd been one hour later, the park authorities would have given away our site.

I helped Dad set up the tent, but that was a Mom thing too. Dad was swearing by the time we put on the fly. Dad never used to swear. Mom sometimes swore when she drove, even if there were no snakes in the car. That was a joke, but probably not a very funny one.

Last night we went to sleep as soon as the tent was up because we'd forgotten the flashlights, so we couldn't read or play cards. This morning we bought lights for each of us, and charcoal for the barbecue, so today we're doing really well.

Dad made burgers for supper tonight, and they were delicious. They were the most expensive kind of burger in the grocery store, called Thick and Juicy Sirloin Patties. Mom used to buy Extra Lean Beef Burgers, which are okay but nowhere near as good as the ones Dad bought. Once Mom bought Cheesy Tuna Fish Burgers. How gross is that?

We had a perfect day on the beach today, swimming and building sandcastles and burying Dad in the sand. Sammy brought his boats and his kites, and all his sand toys. The kid is totally organized for someone insane. Dad and I are like dogs. We hear, "Let's go camping!" and we run to the car. Sammy's like Mom. He packs intelligent things that are actually useful on a beach.

We took his boats into the water and sailed them back to shore about five hundred times. Sammy wore his life jacket in the lake, and he didn't seem too scared. He's not a bad swimmer, but he's afraid to get his face wet, so he'd panic and drown if he didn't have a jacket on. He looks like one of those old ladies you see in swimming pools craning their necks out of the water because they don't want to get their hair wet. They all have the same hairdo, those old ladies— it's always short gray hair in curls. You never see old ladies with straight hair. Never.

The boats sailed away from us once, and we followed them down the beach and saw Karen's mom. She was sitting on a lawn chair reading a magazine. When she saw me she stuck her cigarette in the sand to put it out. There were cigarette butts all around her chair, like a hundred of them poking through the sand. It was totally gross.

I asked her if Karen was here. She said she didn't know where Karen was. I said, "Do you mean you don't know where Karen is on the beach or you don't know where Karen is in the world?" She said, "Where on the beach?" like it was a question. Far off in the water, a girl with brown braids played with a beach ball. It might have been Karen, but she never waved back, so who knows?

I'm going to walk around the campsites tonight to see if I can find her. It's not like I'm stalking her. I just want to know if she's here and if she knows who her homeroom teacher is. School starts on Tuesday.

Simpson's cross-boundary transfer came through, so he'll be at my school this year, even though his mom's house is in a different school district. I went to their new house yesterday before soccer. It's really nice. It's in a new development with no trees and small yards, where you get lost going for a walk because everything looks the same, like a robot made it, and you can't find any landmarks. But once you're locked up tight in the house, it's great. The basement is a giant playroom, with a wide-screen TV and an Xbox. It's too bad it's so far from our house.

Simpson's mom was happy to have me over. She showed me the insides of her kitchen cupboards. Mom used to do that kind of thing, like show me pillows she'd bought for the couch. I'd say, "Mom, I don't care about stuff like that." She'd say, "Josh, I don't care about the attack and defense powers of every *World of Warcraft* hero you ever made, but I still listen politely because it's important to you." That's true— except they're not actually heroes, they're just characters, but the principle's the same. I told Simpson's mom her cupboards were awesome.

Dad's trying to peek at my journal right now. He's faking a stretch, but his eyes are glued to my book. He must have seen the capital *M*, so he knows I'm writing something about Mom. I smiled like it was all good, but he's still trying to peek. I haven't looked at his journal since that one time. I probably should, to find out if he's still so sad. I hope not. At least he knows it wasn't me who put the snake in Mom's car. And it probably wasn't Sammy either.

Sam had a great day today. I haven't seen him so happy in ages. Finally he had some kids to play with. Some of them wanted to steal his toys, but I kept watch. I also stopped Sam from giving all his boats away.

That's the kind of thing he does, thinking everybody's his friend when really they're total strangers.

After the boats, we tried flying Sam's kites, but there wasn't enough wind, and Sammy kept tripping over people when he ran down the beach for takeoff power. We switched to sand castles. Again I was amazed at Sammy's awesome packing skills. Not only did he bring his buckets and shovels, but he brought all his little Pokémon figures too. We made a huge sand coliseum, with Pokémon battles in the center and a Pokémon audience around the sides. Two little five-year-olds helped us build it. They must have been neglected children or something, because their parents went to the canteen for an hour while the kids played with us. Sammy was a totally normal boy with them.

Now we're at our campsite sitting at the picnic table with our journals, using our arms to shield the pages from each other. It's not like we were all having strong emotions. Dad writes in his journal after supper every day, so we're sticking with his schedule. "Taking advantage of the light," Dad called it.

I peeked in Sam's journal, and it looks like he's drawing space stuff. Madame Denis said Space is the September theme for her class. I thought that was amazing, because every other kindergarten teacher I know does Apples in September. Not that I actually know any kindergarten teachers, but every year in September I'd see pictures of apples on display outside the kindergarten classes. Madame Denis sounds like a real trailblazer.

It's good for Sam to put his mind on something besides snakes and dying. Space is an excellent subject. Mom liked space—Sam told Madame Denis that about five thousand times after she said it was their theme.

Once when Mom took us to the Museum of Science and Technology, we went on the Mission to Mars simulator ride three times in a row. We liked it so much the first time that we bought tickets for the next show. It was just as much fun the second time, so we bought more tickets. It wasn't as much fun the third time. The museum was almost empty that day, so we had to save Mars by ourselves, just me and Sammy and Mom. We held hands and screamed and giggled—except by the third time we were forcing the screams because, really, twice was enough.

Mom used to stargaze through a telescope on the back deck until she left it out one night last fall and somebody stole it. Two summers ago she bought me a Star Tracker to teach me the constellations. It came with a book, a CD and a set of binoculars. You're supposed to read the book first, then go out at night with the binoculars and a Walkman to find the constellations. You wear headphones while you search the sky. It seemed kind of dangerous to me, since you can't see or hear anyone on Earth who might be sneaking up on you.

I only tried the Star Tracker for ten minutes. The constellations were too hard to find. They should have connected the stars into simple geometric shapes instead of imagining fancy drawings of guys carrying water buckets that are impossible to see. I only remember the two bears. They don't look like bears, but they're easy to find because they contain the dippers, which actually look like dippers. Karen was impressed when I showed her those constellations back in the spring.

Mom's favorite thing in the night sky was the moon. She always said, "Look at that moon," every time it was full. She said if you loved someone far away, you could look up at the moon and think about them looking at it too, and feel closer to them. I have no idea what she was talking about when she said that, because as far as I know all the people she loved were right in our house.

She said the moon reminded her of how special the Earth is. It has waterfalls and salt flats and oceans and forests, and plants and animals, and colors and noise, instead of just being a cold rock falling through space without making a sound.

In grade five, I did my science project on the moon. I learned about the different forces pulling it toward the Earth and away from the Earth at the same time, just as the Earth is pulled toward the sun and away from the sun at the same time, so everything keeps going around and around. It's pretty amazing. When I made my display, Simpson asked me, "Why doesn't everything just fall through space?" I told him, "Everything *is* falling through space, man. It's just that some things are falling together."

It feels like our lives are like that too. Like we're all falling through space and being pulled in different directions. In our family, Mom was the sun, and the three of us were planets, and we were safe because even though we were pulled away, Mom swung us back with her gravity. She kept us together and happy, not terrified or even noticing that we were falling through endless space. When she died, we were left hurtling through emptiness. There was a real danger that we might shoot off in our own directions—Dad falling one way and Sammy falling another, and me left alone and spinning. For a while it felt like we were lost.

But now I think the three of us are circling each other. Even if we are hurtling through the universe, and even if there is no sun to swing us back, I don't think we're going to fly apart from each other. Maybe we'll be pulled closer together. We felt closer today, when Sam and I buried Dad in the sand. Even now, hiding our journals from each other, it feels like we're closer.

Today was a beautiful day. Sammy took imaginary pictures just about every second. *Snap, snap, snap.*

Sunday, September 2nd

It's Sunday, and we're going home early and I'm writing this in the car. I don't even want to write it down, but I'm afraid I'll remember it wrong later if I don't. I know I'll remember it forever. I just might remember it wrong.

Sammy came with me to check out the campsites last night. We took our new flashlights because it was nearly dark. People were playing their radios so loud, the noise traveled over the whole campground. We swung our lights in time to the music. A song came on with a lonely drumbeat. Someone screamed like it was her favorite song in the world, and she turned the radio up even louder. That sad drum followed me and Sammy past dozens of campsites where couples drank beer, and friends talked around fires, and mothers sat at tables wiping their kids' faces. We walked by all of them to that lonely beat, swinging our lights.

We saw Karen and her mom with another woman and a boy I didn't recognize. They were sitting around a campfire drinking Coke from cans. I stopped walking when I saw them. I felt really sad. I hadn't noticed I was sad before, because it had been such a great day. But when I saw Karen, I knew that somewhere deep down I'd been sad all day, ever since I saw her mom on the beach and the girl in the water who wouldn't wave back.

Karen didn't run away this time. Maybe her mom told her to get a grip. Or maybe she didn't want to spaz out in front of the boy—who turned out to be her cousin. She stood up and came for a walk with me and Sammy. That stupid drum song was still going on, drifting over the trees down the road all the way to the beach.

The beach was bright, even though the sun had just set and it was only a half moon. We turned off our flashlights and took off our shoes and walked in the wet sand. It was cold and slimy, and it creeped me out.

I did all the talking, because Karen didn't have anything to say. Sammy talked to Mom off to the side with his toy. I told Karen about the Darwin Awards

and how funny some of them are, and how I was
waiting to find out if Mom was going to get one.

I told her about Dad building a time machine like
he was smarter than Albert Einstein. Sammy said,
"Daddy's smarter than everyone." He told Karen that
Dad went to his soccer game and his team was going
to win the tournament.

Karen didn't say anything. She looked at Sammy
like he was the saddest thing in the world, when really
he was happy as can be at that moment, thumping
down the beach with his Power Ranger. She whis-
pered to me, "Is he okay?" I said, "I don't know."

I told her about the mourning practices of
different faiths, and how I wish we were Jewish
because it's such an organized religion. I told her
about the Hindu belief that too much mourning is
bad for the dead person's reincarnation. I told her
that Japanese Buddhists say their forty-nine days are
not over if they don't understand how the person they
loved died. I said we were doing okay, me and Sammy
and Dad, but our forty-nine days are not over.

Karen started to cry, and she told me she'd put the
snake in Mom's car. I thought she must be joking. But
she wasn't. She said she was sorry, she never knew
Mom was afraid of snakes. She cried so hard I could
barely understand her. She said she'd been coming
over to my house to show me a snake she'd caught—

probably to throw it at me, but she didn't say that—and she'd seen me leaving the house with Mom. Mom had her keys in her hand, so Karen thought she was about to drive me to soccer practice. She dumped the snake on the passenger seat of Mom's car to scare me when I sat down. But I didn't get in the car. I always skipped Saturday practice. I biked over to the Dungeon to play cards instead.

So the snake wasn't hiding under Mom's seat for days. It was only there for ten seconds before Mom got in the car, and then ten minutes until she hit the highway and saw it.

I didn't have anything to say to Karen when she told me that. She was crying and saying she was sorry. She was really crying her guts out. But when she tried to hug me, I didn't want to touch her. I wanted her to get away from me. Mostly I was confused, like I couldn't understand what she was saying. For one thing, I didn't remember leaving the house at the same time as Mom. I thought I was home with Sammy all day. But no, I biked to the Dungeon. On the way back I met Simpson on the bike path, and he came over to my place. When we rode in, Dad asked Simpson if he would please go home because he had something important to tell me. I'd forgotten all that. That whole morning had disappeared from my head.

That's why I want to write about Karen's "prank" before we get home and I forget what happened last night. I don't want to remember it wrong, like I remembered the morning Mom died. I was sure I remembered sitting in the living room, watching Mom walk out the door—just the way Sammy described her—in her red sundress, her purse falling to her elbow, her hair bouncing off her shoulder, with only a smidgeon of her cheek showing as she walked away from us. But I didn't see her like that. I left the house with her. I saw her face. She looked happy. I remember it clearly now, how she smiled at me and squeezed my hand before she walked to her car.

I even remember biking up the street and waving hello to Karen as I rode past her. She waved back and shouted, "Aren't you getting a ride to practice?" I just blew her a kiss.

I wish so badly that I'd gotten a ride to soccer practice. Or that Karen had run back to Mom's car and taken out the snake. Or I wish she'd never put the snake in the car in the first place. How could she not have known about Mom's phobia? We were friends since grade two! But even if she didn't know, what kind of person puts a snake in someone's car? I could see a fake snake—and maybe even a fake one would have scared Mom to death—but a real snake?

That's a terrible prank to pull. You'd have to be an idiot not to know that was dangerous.

What's funny about putting a snake in someone's car? It's not very funny now. That's what I said to Karen on the beach. She said, "I thought it would be funny." I said, "It's not very funny now."

Then she ran away, probably back to her campfire.

I don't know how long Sammy and I stayed on the beach after that. It was like another freakish time warp. I smashed all the garbage cans with a piece of driftwood. Then I threw the barbecue grates as far as I could into the lake. I picked up every stupid cigarette butt I could find in the sand and ripped them into tiny bits of fluff I wanted to cram down Karen's throat. Sammy grabbed me and said, "Don't cry, Josh, don't cry," until I didn't know what to do. We started to build a sand castle, and eventually Dad came and found us.

Then I yelled at Dad, even though he hadn't done anything wrong. I was just so mad. I yelled that traveling backward in time is impossible and he was an idiot for not knowing that. "Why would you want to time travel anyway?" I yelled. "Wherever you are, you'll always hide from me and Sammy. You've never joined in with us ever in your life! You just waited for Mom to raise us." That was really mean and not actually true, because he'd just let us bury him in the sand and he'd cooked us burgers.

Dad said I was wrong. He said he'd do anything we wanted. Sammy said, "You won't make the Mommy Book." Then Dad said, "Making scrapbooks about your mother is just another way of trying to go back in time." I called him an asshole if he couldn't see the difference between hiding in your basement and sharing stories about someone you love. And I don't usually swear, at least not at home.

I smashed the castle and accidentally kicked sand in Dad's eye. He screamed and swore. I thought we might actually have to go to the hospital, but he had some eyewash in the car. Which is weird, since he forgot the flashlights. I guess he keeps a first-aid kit in his glove compartment.

He didn't have a chance to wash his eye out for almost an hour because I caused another disaster and nearly destroyed Sammy.

Somehow I lost the girl Power Ranger. It was standing on top of the castle when I kicked it down. I must have kicked the Ranger with the sand, way out near the water. Oh my god, Sammy had a fit. I thought it would break my heart, the way he was crying. I buried the toy trying to find it, sweeping away the sand and throwing it on top of the Ranger without knowing it. I couldn't see it anywhere, even with my flashlight. I looked a hundred feet in every direction, and it wasn't there. We all got on our knees, digging and panicking—Dad was searching with just one eye open—until we combed the sand for what felt like forever, scooping right down to where it was dripping wet. But the Ranger was gone.

Sammy made such a creepy frightened wail, screaming, "Where is she? Where is she?" I was afraid that he'd go insane for good, that his mind would just burst from fear and he'd never be okay again. I hugged him and told him, "Everything will be okay," just like all the stupid grown-ups say when it's not actually true, they just want it so badly. I told him we'd never leave that beach until we found it.

Then all of a sudden Dad found it. He stood up and walked away from us to look at the moon and cry, and he stepped right on it. We cheered like he'd found the cure for cancer or stopped a nuclear war or traveled back in time and saved Mom.

It was crazy. We jumped up and down and laughed and hugged. It was the hysterical kind of laughter that can turn into crying at any second. I think sometimes that's the only way I'll ever laugh again. Every time I laugh, I can feel deep down at the bottom of the laugh there's crying, and I could go there at any moment.

Sammy was so happy when Dad passed him the Ranger. He kept repeating, "Daddy found her, Daddy found her," and wiping his eyes and smiling, with his face all wet and blotchy. Then he asked out of the blue,

"Can I go to soccer tomorrow?" Dad started giggling. He said, "Okay. Yeah. We'll leave early."

We packed up the tent this morning, and now we're on our way home.

It's weird, but I slept well last night even though I was so sad and angry about Karen. At least I know what happened. It's even stupider than all the things I thought might have happened, but at least I know. I don't want to see Karen again. Not ever. I know she didn't mean for Mom to die, but I just don't like her anymore.

I can't see us even talking again with that horrible thing between us. Even if I didn't blame her—but I do, because it's obviously her fault—my liking her has disappeared. It disappeared the second she told me she'd put the snake in Mom's car. She was crying so hard, and I could see that she was really sorry, but I didn't care. I just didn't care about her anymore. A switch flipped inside my heart. On. Off.

That's sad, because I really liked liking her. But I just don't like her anymore.

Monday, September 3rd

There are two things I want to write about today. First of all, we won our soccer tournament this weekend. Usually we win all summer but lose the tournament because I'm away camping. Not to brag, but I'm the top scorer in my age group in the whole region. My coaches are always upset when I miss the tournament. Last year the coach said I couldn't sign up in April unless I could guarantee I'd play on Labor Day weekend. So Mom said, "Oh yes, he'll be here." Then she winked at me. Really, how could they force me to go?

There was always something cool about being missed, but man, I'm so glad I went this time. The coach jumped up and down when he saw me on the field. He said, "I guess you didn't go camping because your

mom died," with a big smile on his face. Then he realized what a moronic thing that was to say, and he
apologized. I told him we came home early because
two nights in a falling-down tent with no campfire
was enough fun for this year. And for every year after,
unless Dad finds Sammy a new mom who can build
fires and pack properly.

About a hundred divorced women tried to pick
Dad up at the tournament. That should be against the
mourning rules of all religions. One woman sat so
close to him that I wanted to bean her with the soccer
ball. I guess widowers are exciting compared to all the
pathetic divorced dads in the world. Dad was wearing
shorts and sunglasses, and he didn't look as zoned out
as usual. He looked smart—which he is, despite his
attempt to build a time machine.

I went down to the basement this morning and
looked under the tarp. His machine is made from
a do-it-yourself airplane kit you can buy for eight
hundred dollars. How is that going to fly fast enough
to travel through time? I asked Dad about it, and he
said, "That's not my only material, Josh." Like he has
a secret stash of antimatter just behind the curtain.
I can tell he still thinks he could build it if he just
kept tinkering. I hope he doesn't try. There's no such
thing as time travel. You're always here and now,
and you just have to deal with it. Even if you got

somewhere else, once you were there it would be here and now.

It would be amazing if Mom were with us here and now. I can't explain how much I would like that to happen. But I know it can't. If she could see us here and now, she'd want us to be happy. She wouldn't want Dad to flirt with other women at my games though. She'd want a good solid year of mourning, with her tree decorated on her birthday and the scrapbooks to keep forever.

I'm not so sure about the memory jewelry. I took off her necklace for soccer because it's pretty dangly and a bit girly after all. I might stick with just the watch. Maybe one day if I like another girl, I'll give the tree necklace to her. But if she pulls a sicko prank, I'm taking it back.

Sammy's macaroni necklace broke during his soccer game. The string came untied and all the macaronis slipped off. He'd forgotten that he was wearing it as a memory of Mom, so he just laughed. Then he and his teammates stomped all the noodles like it was great fun.

He carried the girl Power Ranger through his whole game. I don't think we have any hope of transferring Mom's memory to anything else. He'll just carry that Ranger until one day he stops. That's not so bad. People make allowances for kids who lose

their mother. Probably for years they'll make allowances for Sammy.

He's here in my bed right now, fast asleep. I don't
think his forty-nine days are over yet. He never cared
how the snake got in Mom's car, so knowing how
doesn't explain anything for him. It does for me—
I don't know why, but it feels like a weight off my
mind. I still ask, "Why didn't she just pull over?"
That's something I'll never know, because I'll never
understand phobias. You'd think evolution would
have weeded them out. In my game, *Evolution*,
I'm going to include a phobia or two that gets
weeded out.

I can't believe I just wrote that. That means I think
Mom deserves a Darwin Award.

But she would want her phobia weeded out of
the gene pool. She didn't want me and Sammy to fear
snakes. It bothered her that I'm afraid of them.

There was a snake on the path to the cow field
during my soccer game. Sammy wandered off again
and saw it. He got excited the way he used to, like he
was thrilled to find it. Then he stopped suddenly as
if a light went on in his head, reminding him that a
snake killed Mom. He didn't know what to do. Dad
walked up beside him and said it would make Mom
happy to see Sam excited about a snake, and that
she'd be sad if he hurt it.

It made me realize that the snake that killed Mom must have died in the car crash. It must have been squashed, and that's how they knew it was in the car. That would have made Mom sad. She never liked for animals to die, not even snakes.

Sammy and Dad watched the snake until it noticed them and slithered away. I wasn't there—Dad told me about it later. He said it could be the story to end our scrapbook with. He said he was sorry for saying the books were as stupid as his time machine—only he didn't put it in those words—but he'd wanted to warn us not to get lost in our memories. Says the guy who spent the past two months in the basement with home movies and a time machine. I didn't backtalk this time, because I knew what Dad meant. For a while I liked the scrapbooks so much that I wanted to put everything in them, every conversation Mom ever had and every single thing she ever did. You could get totally lost doing that. It could take over my life without ever bringing hers back. So I know what Dad meant. And he's right—Sammy watching the snake while I win the soccer tournament is a perfect story to end our book.

We were the soccer champions, and I was the lead scorer again this year. I got a medal of honor. Sammy's team won their first game in the tournament, but they lost the second game. Sam didn't know the difference.

He sort of scored in the first game, and he was very happy and proud. It wasn't actually during game time, but Sammy didn't know that. The other team's goalie didn't know either, because he tried hard to stop the shot. Chloe gave Sam a high five afterward—so everyone thought it was a goal. Since the coach practically ripped the shirt off his daughter's back to let Sam on the field, he wasn't about to say, "That goal doesn't count!" It was a good goal, and Sam will probably be a good soccer player when he's older.

Simpson and his mom came out for dinner with us after the tournament. She showed off an earring she bought for the new hole in her ear—she took the bandage off a few days ago. Simpson was proud of his piercing. But I don't know, it still looks unhealthy to me. It's not bleeding or scabbed anymore, but it's freakishly white, like the whole ear might fall off at any second.

Dad said it looked great, and maybe he should get his ear pierced too. I laughed my head off to think of Dad with an earring. He said he used to wear rings in both his ears when he was young. I find that impossible to believe.

Sammy told the only ring joke he knows, which is also a space joke. I told it to him after we met his kindergarten teacher and learned that he'd be studying space. Right there in the restaurant, right on cue after Dad bragged about his earrings, Sammy turned to Dad with a smile and said, "I know there's a ring around Saturn, but is there a ring around Uranus?" Then he cracked up. So did I, because it was pretty funny coming from a four-year-old. And so did Simpson's mom, because I guess she never heard that joke before.

It turned out to be an okay weekend after all, except it felt like a month instead of just three days. Today Sammy and I walked to the park, but Karen was there, and so were Darren and his mom, so we just kept walking down to the bike path. I half expected Sam to run back and take another shot at Darren, but he didn't. I had to stop myself from running back to take a shot at Karen too. I had a vision of myself chasing her down, the way Sam had chased Darren, and pummeling her face to a pulp. But I snapped out of it and just kept walking. Karen waved at me when we passed. I didn't wave back. I knew I should wave to be polite, but my arm wouldn't lift up.

I don't feel anything about Karen now. I'm not very mad or sad about her today. I'm sad that I stopped liking her, but relieved too. Maybe there'll be some new girls I like in junior high. Girls who don't pull pranks and kill people.

There's an online grieving group that says people with no faith need to make up their own mourning rituals, like we've been doing. They suggest writing a letter to the dead person and then burning it to send the words up to the person's spirit. I thought that might be nice to do, especially since Mom wanted to be burned. But since she's buried, maybe we should write a letter and bury it. I don't know. Maybe we'll just finish the scrapbooks and decorate the tree

School starts tomorrow, and I'm way behind on the chores and I need to simplify. That's what Mom used to say when people called to ask for help and she didn't have time. She'd say, "I'm sorry, but I can't take on any more projects right now. I need to simplify." Then she'd hang up the phone and do a little dance and go rent a movie.

It's hard to believe it's only been sixty-five days since she died. I guess that's too long to count by days, so I should just say two months. One day I'll count it by years. Then eventually I won't even count it. I'll just say, "My mother died when I was twelve." And it will be such a distant memory it'll be like a fact in history. That's so sad to imagine.

I called Professor Johnston today. Mitchell. He wasn't there because it's a holiday, but I left a message on his machine—which he remembered to change, thank god, because it's Mom's old number. As I was dialing, I thought, What if the machine answers and it's still Mom's voice? Then I'd spend the whole day on the phone, and Sammy and Dad would ask what I was doing, and we'd all end up listening to Mom's message a million times until Mitchell took out a restraining order on us. But anyway, he'd changed the recording, so that didn't happen.

In my message, I thanked him for telling me about the Einstein exhibit. I said I'd been to see it and that Dad had stopped building his time machine. Cheetah probably told Mitchell about seeing me there, and how sad I was afterward, but I didn't want Mitchell to feel bad for telling me to go. He'll be glad to hear that I'm okay now, and that Dad is parenting us better. I also told him we planted Mom's tree, and I thanked him for the idea. I made it a good-bye message, because I don't want him to think of me and Sammy hanging here like desperate orphans. I asked him to say hello to Cheetah for me—that didn't fit with the good-bye theme, but I wouldn't mind seeing her again.

I just read over this entry. I started it with two things to say, and the first thing was soccer, but now I forget what the second thing was. My head is still losing stuff. I better go to sleep now, because we have to get up early for school. I have my lunch packed and my new clothes all ready. Dad found them in his closet tonight and laid them out on my bed. When Sammy came in, he shouted, "Mom got you new clothes too!" He was all happy for me.

Thursday, September 6th

The Darwin Society finally sent me an e-mail. They're not considering Mom for an award. They said Mom would only qualify if she'd known the snake was in the car, like if she'd taken a job transporting snakes even though she was phobic. So that's good news. She wasn't astoundingly stupid at all.

I read online that there are over 2,800 road accident deaths in Canada every year. I found a website full of photographs of car accidents. The whole point of the site is to show mangled cars and dead people. It has captions like "massive fatal crash" and "serious head injury," as if car crashes are totally awesome. I didn't stay on that site, because that's just wrong. A lot more wrong than the Darwin Awards, which are at least funny and not gross. I was worried there might be a picture of Mom's car on the crash site, but I didn't look. It's time to move forward. Not away from Mom, but away from worrying about how stupidly she died.

She would agree with what I just wrote. If she knew she was going to die freaking out over a snake in her car, she'd have admitted it was stupid. Then she'd have asked, "How on earth would a snake get in my car?" That's the most seriously stupid thing of all.

Karen is in two of my classes this year, drama and geography. I sat on the other side of the room from her in both classes. She could tell that she better not try to talk to me.

Simpson is in all of my classes, which is awesome. Turner is in all of them too. Ameer is only in geography and gym, but there's an after-school computer course we're going to take together. He'll probably make the soccer team with me and Simpson, so I'll still see him a lot.

The first few days of school have been all right—it's great seeing my friends and having something to do all day—but man, I'm tired. I almost fell asleep in English this morning. I was used to sleeping in and drifting through the days. Hurrying is totally out of character for me now. I manage to make the bus every morning. Dad sets the alarm and gets me out of bed in time to have a shower. My clothes are usually wrinkled but they're acceptable colors, so I've been looking pretty good.

For English we had to write a page about ourselves and our summer. I was dreading that. I thought of totally lying, but I didn't. I wrote that my mom was killed in a car accident the day before Canada Day, so my family was in mourning all summer. I wrote that we'll be in mourning for a year, but next July we'll go see the fireworks and our mourning will be over—except it won't be, because every time a really good firework goes off, I'll wish Mom was there to see it. It just came to me in class how that should be our ritual. Sammy and I love fireworks, and because they're at night, Dad won't be able to read through them.

That's a joke, and I didn't put it in my English paper.

School is good so far, but Sammy and I really have to get to bed earlier. The first morning Sam was like a zombie. He'd forgotten basic hygiene routines like how to brush his teeth. When Dad asked, "Did you brush your teeth yet?" Sam looked at him like he was speaking Russian. I guess he didn't brush his teeth all summer. That's disgusting, but I never really noticed at the time.

Sammy's a total whiner at breakfast because he got used to eating waffles at eleven o'clock every day through the summer. Five minutes to wolf down cereal is a shock for him. But he made his bus. It's a different bus from mine. It comes half an hour earlier. The first day of school, I woke up with him because I wasn't sure Dad could handle it. But Dad was already awake, so I slept in a bit. Sammy whined over that, until we reminded him that his bus comes home earlier than mine too. That's when we realized Sammy would be getting off the school bus at three o'clock and no one would be here to meet him. Dad called the school in a panic. They said Sam was enrolled in after-school daycare, so Dad can pick him up after work. Even when she's dead, Mom thinks of everything. I don't tell Sam she'd arranged it when she registered him for kindergarten last year. It makes him smile to think of her making phone calls from Heaven.

Sam loves school so much he won't shut up about it. He already knows the names of every kid in his class, and he calls them all "*mon ami.*" Nobody is just "David" or "Jacob." They're "*mon ami* David" and "*mon ami* Jacob." He loves his teacher, Madame Denis. When I told him that Pluto isn't a planet anymore, he freaked out because Madame Denis says it is. Most adults are totally unaware of any scientific advances that have occurred since they left university.

Sammy loves daycare too, because it's two solid hours of fun. His first day there, he made a giant sombrero with cut-out butterflies all over it, and it's been on his head ever since. He just ran into my room wearing it. Now he's bouncing on my bed, holding the blue Ranger, looking like the happiest kid in the world. Cleo must have sensed him coming, because she slunk away before he got here. The cats haven't trusted him since the dress-up incident.

Sam told his ring-around-Uranus joke to Madame Denis on the first day of school. She sent a note home to Dad about it. She obviously has Dad labeled as a neglectful parent. The next day she wrote a note saying that Sam was a good student and very helpful to his classmates. It could be the truth, or it could be that Sammy started talking about his dead mother and Madame Denis felt bad about the first note.

Sam goes to school and daycare with Chloe across the street, and they're best friends now. Chloe's dad, Mr. Simpson-is my-*last*-name, is going to share daycare pickups with Dad. He feels so sorry for Sammy that he'll probably invite him to dinner every night. So instead of Dad finding Sam a new mom, Sammy has found a whole new family.

I better have my friends over to the house often this year. If Sammy's across the street and I'm at a friend's house, Dad will be all alone. That's just sad. He's being a good dad now. He waits with Sam for the bus and packs him a good lunch—not pasta salad and chicken drumsticks, but a ham sandwich with grapes and Pringles and peanut-free granola bars.

He did something totally awesome for me and Sammy this week. He scanned photographs and downloaded pictures and digitized the home movies and made an amazing electronic map with his work software.

It starts with a map of the world, with cities you can zoom in on, like London and Orlando and Montreal. You click on a section of town to see the streets. When you click on a street you get a picture of Mom with a story of what she did there. It's like a huge computer game—there are a thousand pages of pictures and stories and movie clips. It's a map of Mom's life with us.

You can click on the hospital and get pictures of me and Sammy when we were just born, and the nurses who delivered us, and news clips of what was going on that day. You can click on different buildings at the university and get stories from Mom's friends, like Cheetah and Mitchell. There's nothing about the stalker guy though, because I looked.

On our street, the map gets busy with pictures of practically all the neighbors. Even Karen—because I hadn't told Dad what she did yet. There's a map of our yard, with pictures of the garden and the cats and our old dog, Kiwi, who really was alive when I was a baby—there's a picture of us together.

It has a virtual tour of our house, so you can circle around each room. If you click on the front door, you see me when I'm one year old pushing a carriage into the screen—which is how I asked to go outside before I learned to speak.

In the map of my room, you can click the TV and get a picture of all my video games. Then if you click *Final Fantasy X*, there's a picture of me when I was eight years old and a story about how it took me three weeks to beat the third transformation of Seymour. Or if you click *Scooby-Doo! Mystery Mayhem*, there's a movie of me holding the controller and laughing while Sammy hides his eyes in my armpit.

Dad said he wanted the map to be a memorial of family life with Mom. So there's a lot about me and Sammy in it. I was totally surprised, because I never thought Dad was paying attention to us all these years. I had no idea he knew where I stashed my Halloween candy.

Maybe Dad knows more than he lets on. And maybe his job's not so boring after all, if he can make something so totally awesome in just a week. He could probably help me with my *Evolution* game.

When Dad clicked on Karen's house in the map of our street, I didn't say anything for a while. I'd been trying to ignore that part of the map. Dad clicked on it, and up popped a picture of me in Karen's yard when we were nine years old. Dad said, "Look at you two," like he thought it would make me happy. The picture showed me and Karen in the winter, building a snowman with her parents, who weren't divorced yet. We were all smiling and pink from the cold. We looked like a family, as if Karen and I were brother and sister. I'm so glad we're not—how awful would that be? I stared at the picture for a minute without talking, just looking at her face. She looked young and happy, like she could never do a bad thing in her life. Dad asked me why I was crying. So I told him that Karen put the snake in Mom's car.

He was shocked and confused at first, like I'd been. He asked what she was doing on our property, which I thought was a weird thing to ask. He asked how I knew it was her, so I told him about the night at the beach. Then he left the house.

For a while I thought maybe he'd gone up the street to kill Karen in revenge. He looked ready to explode when he left. He did go to her house, but he didn't kill her. He just yelled at her. And at her mother. He told me he made them both cry—which isn't nice, but really, they ought to do a little crying. After all, we've cried for the past two months, and we'll cry for the rest of our lives. I don't know exactly what Dad said to them, but he came home all yelled out and cried out and pretty much a mess.

I told him I was sorry, and that if I'd just gone to my soccer practice in the car, Mom would never have died that day. I started bawling. Dad hugged me and said, "It's not your fault, Josh." I blew my nose and said, "I guess it's nobody's fault." Then Dad said, "It's Karen's fault." We looked at each other and laughed in a crying sort of way. I said, "I always hated her mother." Dad said, "Me too." And we laughed and cried some more. Then Dad erased their house from the map of Mom's life.

I think Dad is starting to live in reality again. There's nothing like a good dose of anger to push you out of the denial stage of grief. Even though we're not Jewish and we have no guidelines to help us mourn, I think we're moving forward. It's not like we're walking away from Mom. I'll never let myself do that. It's more like we're keeping her with us, but without getting stuck at the place in the path where she died.

I know my whole life will be different without her, all because of those few stupid decisions that led to the accident. I'm so sad about that, and I miss her. That's all there is to say. I miss her. I wish she were here so I could make her laugh, and she could be proud of me. And maybe she could put Sammy in his own bed so I could stretch out for a change.

I checked back over this journal tonight, like Dr. Tierney suggested, but there weren't a lot of strong emotions in it. Maybe I'm more like Dad than I realize. I didn't write every day, but the scrapbook has taken a lot of our time. It's going to be totally awesome.

I know I can't keep Mom's life in a book. I can't even keep my own life in my head. Like the way I forgot leaving the house the day she died. How could I forget something like that? There must be a million things my head won't hold. I'm putting the best things in the Mom Book, to hold them there in case I forget. It's different from Dad's map, because it's mine and Sam's. When we look at it years from now, we'll think, *Wow. We were just kids when we made this. That's totally amazing. We must have loved her so much.*

We've started gluing in the pictures and writing out stories that go with them. We're not using the paper Karen's mom gave us. We're drawing our own captions and borders. I put in some of Mom's jokes here and there, with cut-out pictures of her face and little speech bubbles for the words.

Sammy wants to put in knock-knock jokes that are four hundred years old. Like "Knock-knock." "Who's there?" "Hatch." "Hatch who?" "Bless you."

And "Knock-knock." "Who's there?" "Lettuce." "Lettuce who?" "Let us in, it's cold outside." Which is totally stupid in the middle of summer. The only knock-knock joke that was actually Mom's was the rude one, "Knock-knock." "Who's there?" "Gope." "Gope who?" "No, I don't have to." You only get it if you say it out loud.

Even without the knock-knock jokes, it's going to take up four giant scrapbooks. It's a bit long, but really, it's a whole lifetime, so what do you expect?

Acknowledgments

Thanks to my editor, Sarah Harvey, for supporting this book so enthusiastically. Special thanks to my son, Sawyer Austen, for proofreading the original manuscript. And thanks to my husband, Geoff, for paying the bills while I wrote it.

Catherine Austen lives in Quebec with her husband, Geoff, and their children, Sawyer and Daimon. *Walking Backward* is her first novel.